Gregg Olsen / Waters Edge

Cassidy - U of O volcanologist
Reeve - ~~half brother~~ step brother
Rebecca - step sister

RESCUING REEVE

BOOK 1 IN THE CASSIDY KINCAID
MYSTERY SERIES

Quinn - Cassidy's biological brother
Bruce - tour leader
Mel -
Phil - Cassidy's husband

D1738002

next story series
Riley Stone / FBI agent
missing persons

author
→ hendles Elliot / small town sheriff
tough but vulnerable

Copyright © 2018 by Amy Waeschle. All rights reserved.

Publisher: Savage Creek Press

Genre: Adult Mystery, Women's Detective.

All Rights Reserved. No part of this book may be used or reproduced in any manner whatsoever without the expressed written permission of the author.

This is a work of fiction. While, as in all fiction, the literary perceptions and insights are based on experience, all names, characters, places, and incidents either are products of the author's imagination or are used fictitiously.

ISBN: 9781070174020

Editor: Jana Stojadinović

Cover Photograph: Shutterstock

Cover Design: Coverluv

Author Photo: Josh Monthei

For my surf sisters,
thank you for your
inspiration, your laughter,
and for sharing the journey

To Ann,
So great to reconnect
and so lovely to share
Meg's journey

Amy Wade

ONE

VOLCÁN ARENAL, COSTA RICA

CASSIDY DIDN'T CONSIDER her job dangerous. Yes, volcanoes spewed lava and toxic fumes, but she knew how to be safe. She understood how to read a mountain's signals.

She was not so skilled when it came to reading people, something that had gotten her in trouble more than once. Could that be the source of her persistent unease all day? It certainly wasn't the fear of an imminent eruption. Her research revealed no such threat.

And it definitely wasn't this morning's unanswered text from her stepsister, Rebecca: If you're still in Costa Rica, please reply. Urgent.

Rebecca's idea of "urgent" was very different than Cassidy's. Rebecca probably wanted to remind Cassidy to buy plane tickets for their Christmas gathering. Didn't Rebecca know that Cassidy was in the field, working like a dog to gather every last scrap of data, important research that could save people's lives?

"Try it now," Héctor, her field tech and indispensable fixer, called from the nearby seismic station that they had built from a car battery, various cables, and a very expensive seismometer.

Cassidy flipped her braid over her shoulder and stomped on the cindery ground to make a mini earthquake. The digital waveform on her laptop jumped, and then she watched the GPS record the station's time and coordinates.

"Woohoo!" she cried. After setting up two of these stations on Arenal that day, she was grubby, her fingertips raw from digging in the volcanic soil, her brow salty from sweat. A cold beer and a shower were now just a jeep ride away.

She and Héctor carefully buried the Pelican box containing the now-working kit just as the setting sun washed the barren hillside with a golden glow. Cassidy took a moment to close her eyes and let the moment sink in, a moment she would have shared immediately with Pete if he was still alive.

All stations up and running, she would have texted him.

He would have texted back: *Nice! Is the volcano behaving herself?*

Yes, unlike me. I plan to get drunk and eat too many empanadas.

"There's dancing tonight," Héctor said in his melodic accent. She sometimes caught him singing as they hiked to and from her stations. Despite his engineering training, he was far from nerdy. He had a charismatic smile and always found ways to make her laugh. Her stomach quivered—that same unease firing again.

"Are you going?" she asked.

He was leaning on handle of the shovel, a playful look in his brown eyes. The idea took her by surprise. *Dancing?*

"I think everyone ees going," he said.

By *everyone*, he would've meant their team of seven: a mix of techs like himself, local scientists, government researchers, and University of Oregon academics like herself.

"Then I guess I'm going, too," she said.

ON THE JEEP ride down the rocky, pockmarked road, she caught Héctor glance at the gold band she was spinning around her left ring finger.

"How long will you wear it?" he asked her quietly.

Cassidy's face burned, and a gut-twisting sensation made her feel suddenly sick. She stayed focused on the road. Pete had been gone for just over a year—a year that she had not known how to survive. The anniversary of his passing had come and gone almost three weeks ago, a night she had spent holed up in her small house, waiting for something different to happen, or simply to feel different, though whether she expected it to be better or worse, she didn't know. She had cried, drank one cocktail—a ginger beer, rum, and lime concoction, his favorite—worn his faded, blue hoody, the one that no longer held his scent, and reread the only two cards she had thought to save. One was from a care package he had sent her when she was doing fieldwork on Mt. St. Helens, the other from her birthday two years ago. These things were all she had left of him, besides the ring, a gold band etched with an endless wave and inset with tiny sparks of peridot, a volcanic gem, placed just above the peaks to look like phosphorescence or stars.

"I don't know," she said, after swallowing a dry lump in her throat.

Héctor went back to humming the Garth Brooks tune that had been playing on the radio that afternoon.

THE SHOWER RAN cold after five minutes, but Cassidy didn't care. It felt good compared to the stuffy humidity of the hotel room; plus, she knew she would just start sweating the minute she stepped out of the shower. *Might as well enjoy five more minutes of not feeling like a baked turkey.*

Her phone chirped from the nightstand, and the memory of her imagined text to and from Pete sent a jolt through her heart. Figuring it was only her colleague, Dennis, telling her where to meet for dinner, she ignored it until she had dried off and dressed in faded cotton shorts and a button-down linen shirt. When she checked her phone—the screen's waterproof case so scratched that it was hard to read in certain kinds of light—below Dennis's expected text, she saw the unanswered one from Rebecca.

If you're still in Costa Rica, please reply. Urgent.

Cassidy and Rebecca had connected on WhatsApp before Cassidy's first trip to Central America two years ago. Rebecca was like that—she wanted a way to reach Cassidy in an emergency. As if any emergency of Reb's would be an emergency of hers.

That same twinge sparked in her gut. Talking to Rebecca was never easy—since Cassidy's father died, she had tried to distance herself from her stepfamily. And since Pete's accident, these strained relationships had become especially hard to manage.

Cassidy decided to reply to Rebecca in the morning, when she was fresh.

During a lively dinner at their favorite hangout, Cassidy enjoyed several beers, knowing that she didn't need her mental faculties in place in order to fix broken field equipment later that night. After dinner, she and her colleagues walked to the club.

La Fortuna was a small town, but some nights there was music, and tonight a salsa band was pumping out melodies from inside the fenced stage. They paid the entrance fee, bought beers, and shuffled through a dark hallway to the open-air plaza. The loud horns and rich voices, along with a heavy beat, thumped into the crowded space. About half were locals; the other half were a mix of Arenal volcano tourists and a few other scientists from Cassidy's team.

To Cassidy's surprise, Elizabeth, a postdoc from the University of Washington, accepted the hand of Eduardo, a researcher from the local observatory, and they disappeared into the throng. She watched them move in time to the beat and wondered where Elizabeth had learned to salsa dance. Cassidy bobbed in time with the beat, and the others in her group did variations of this, sipping their beers and chatting in loud voices over the music. Héctor was laughing with Dennis, a postdoc from Cambridge, but caught her eye. Cassidy looked away.

A moment later, he was at her side. "Let's go, *profesora*," he said, his hand at her back.

"I can't," Cassidy said, her body rigid. In graduate school, she and two friends had taken a Latin dance class, but she had never used it.

Pete didn't know how, and they had never gotten around to trying it together. Just one of the many things they hadn't had the time to do.

"I teach you," he said in his rich voice, his lips close to her ear. She watched him for a moment, took in his curly brown hair that was touched with a few strands of gray at the temples, his solid, trim body. At that moment, his smile was warm, mischievous. She had known Héctor since her first trip to Arenal. He was strong, had an easy laugh, and could fix anything. Her pause must have signaled acquiescence because he led her out to the dance floor.

THE NEXT MORNING, Cassidy lay awake, listening to the geckos chirp softly for some time before the dawn. It might have been the squall that had woke her or the distant thunder. Of course sleep wouldn't come easy. It never did. The memory of dancing with Héctor lingered in her mind and she tried to savor it, take it for what it was—a lovely, sweet moment with a friend. He had lingered at the restaurant, making it clear he would walk her home, but she gracefully turned him down.

She slipped out of bed, moved to the window, and opened the wide, wooden slats. Her hotel room had no view, only a partial of the street outside and the jungle, which extended to Arenal's black, bald cone. Dawn wasn't far off—she knew that because the frog song was fading, and the half moon, free of the clouds, hovered low in the sky.

A sudden glow lit up a small area of the floor, where she had deposited her shorts—too tired last night to undress properly. The glow came from her phone, which displayed another text from Rebecca. She slipped on her glasses and read the message:

Q told me you're still in CR. It's about Reeve. I think he's in trouble. Has he called you?

Of course Rebecca had called Quinn, Cassidy's biological brother and best friend.

Cassidy slumped onto the bed and set the phone down, a heavy sense of guilt at not taking Rebecca seriously the night before settling into her gut.

Reeve.

Her stepbrother and perennial screw-up. *I think he's in trouble.*

Cassidy gazed through the window's slats again to pale pink hues weaving into the jungle. She sighed, her shoulders dropping in resignation.

When wasn't Reeve in trouble?

There was no way to ignore this. If Reeve was in Costa Rica, and needing rescue, she would help. Even though she'd tried and failed so many times before. Even though Reeve likely didn't want her help.

The idea that Reeve may have called her was especially alarming. He never called her—the last time she had seen him, a police officer was shoving him into the back of a patrol car.

Cassidy scrolled through her WhatsApp call log. She remembered vaguely that Reeve had been in Costa Rica for about a year, doing what, she didn't know. Hopefully, getting his life together. Her log was full of correspondence with her CR team, as she had readied for her trip down, details she had been coordinating for weeks before her travel. Then, she saw it: a call from Reeve on October 5th at 9:18 p.m. No message.

Cassidy's skin pricked with goose bumps.

So Reeve *had* tried to reach her—after more than a year of silence. Cassidy suppressed a shiver. Reeve never called unless he wanted something, or he was in trouble.

The dangerous kind.

TWO

CASSIDY TRIED CALLING Rebecca a third time, but with no luck. Ironically, she would have had better reception in the field, but she had returned the keys to the jeep and packed up her equipment, dirty field boots, tool bag, and field notebooks.

Her team had already dispersed, leaving her free to board her bus for the coast without guilt for taking a few extra days for a surf trip.

Finally, two hours later when Cassidy's bus stopped in Cañas, Rebecca picked up on the second ring.

"What the hell, Cass?" she said, sounding breathless.

Cassidy squinted down the bright, dusty street. The moist, super-heated air of midday was making her sweat, but it felt good compared to the frigid air-conditioned bus.

"Reception sucks, okay?" Cassidy answered. "I've been trying all morning."

Rebecca made a dramatic huff on her end. "I can't get a hold of Reeve," she said.

"He did call me," Cassidy said. A stubborn grain of guilt was hitching her progress towards being aloof. Like a burr stuck in a sock on a long hike—all she had to do was ignore it, and the thing would eventually work itself out.

Why would Reeve call her?

"When?" Rebecca gasped.

"Last month."

The line buzzed with silence, and Cassidy knew what Rebs was thinking because she was thinking it, too. That Reeve wouldn't just call to say hello.

"I haven't heard from him since then. He checks in."

"What's he doing down here?" Cassidy asked. It wasn't like she and Reeve talked. Ever. Cassidy got all her news from Rebecca.

"He's in some surfing town," Rebecca said. "Maybe you've heard of it."

Cassidy shuffled her feet, and the grit beneath her flip-flops scraped against the sidewalk. She leaned against the outer wall of the Supermercado, where an advertisement for a drink called Tropical was painted in bright blue, yellow, and green.

"Which town," Cassidy sighed, picturing her version of post-field work R&R—five days of surfing uncrowded waves and lounging by a gorgeous pool—bursting into flames.

"Tamarindo," Rebecca said slowly, as if she was reading it. "Is that anywhere near you?"

"No," Cassidy lied.

"Come on, Cassidy," Rebecca replied. In the background, a baby began to scream, and Cassidy could hear Rebecca moving swiftly, then her calming, chirpy mommy voice soothing the baby with some kind of nonsense language. So it was Lyle, her youngest.

"If you gotta go, we can talk later," Cassidy said, doing her best to not sound hopeful.

The child made some kind of snuffling noise, like it was sucking on something. Cassidy wondered if the something was Rebecca.

"No, it's okay," she said in a voice that was halfway between her cooing sweet voice and the bark she usually deployed on Cassidy.

"Can you just go and ask around in Tamarindo? He was working on some kind of boat. Something to do with surf tours."

Cassidy sighed. Reeve was probably high off his gourd somewhere, his phone stolen or lost, and oblivious that Rebecca was distraught with worry.

"I'll ask around, but I've only got five days left, and I'm not going to spend them pulling him out of whatever hole he's stuck in."

"He might really be in trouble, Cass."

Cassidy sighed a long, slow breath, but it only deepened her guilt. Reeve had stolen from her, threatened her, lied to her. There were moments when she had hated him, but her father had loved him, had tried so hard to help him. Deep down Cassidy knew that she cared for him, too. He just made it so hard to sometimes.

"Okay," she said. "I'll see what I can find out."

CASSIDY HAD to wait for a different bus, and the trip was longer, so she didn't arrive in the surf mecca of Tamarindo until well after dark. She had no idea where to look for Reeve and had no place to stay. From the bus stop, she shouldered her backpack and walked down the dirt road. Music and lights from the open-air restaurants spilled out onto the street. Cassidy peered into each as she passed. A mixture of young backpackers, couples, or families were eating, or playing pool, or at the bar watching TV. At a place called Crazy Mike's Surf Camp, she noticed a typical surfer crowd: young guys in loose T-shirts and board shorts, sitting at the bar or hunched over giant plates of food.

She didn't see anyone who looked like Reeve but didn't expect to. By the time she reached the end of the street, her shoulders, worn out from five hard days of schlepping loads of gear all over the mountain, were aching, and she was soaked with sweat. At a roundabout, the street made a sharp turn to the left, away from the beach. The soft *shushhhh* of waves breaking on the shore drifted through a gap in the storefronts; she followed a path to the cocoa-brown sand and sat down in a tired heap. Another wave crashed on the shore, a pearly white mash in the soft glow coming from the businesses lining it. Offshore, the lights from fishing boats blinked in and out of focus on the black expanse of ocean.

Where would Reeve have hung out, worked? Rebecca had said something about a surf tours business involving a boat. Cassidy groaned, realizing that she would need to return to the surfer hangout and brave its testosterone-scented atmosphere. She could visit other businesses, too, but Crazy Mike's had the right vibe: party.

The gnats had found her ankles, and her stomach was empty. With a sigh, she decided to walk back on the beach. Maybe the town would feel different to her from that perspective.

At the surf camp, she threaded the handful of outside tables full of surfers enjoying nachos or cocktails and peanuts, found the brightly lit bar and slid onto a stool, dropping her grubby pack to the tiled floor. The bartender, a tall, forty-something gringo with a thick blonde ponytail tied at the nape of his neck and quick blue eyes, pushed off the bar and approached her. He tossed down a coaster that landed perfectly between her hands, which were perched on the bar like parentheses.

"What can I get you?" he asked.

"*Una cerveza, por favor,*" she said. Even though it was obvious that English was the language of choice in Crazy Mike's, after her week on the mountain, Spanish flowed just as easily as English. Plus, she wanted some way to communicate that she wasn't some hapless tourist.

The bartender raised an eyebrow, and then brought her an Imperial, cracking the lid on a hidden opener behind the bar before setting it down. "*Tienes hambre, querida?*"

It was Cassidy's turn to raise an eyebrow. *Querida* was a term of mild endearment. She nodded and a menu appeared. After a quick scan, she ordered a chicken burrito.

A pair of college-aged guys tramped through the bar, dripping wet and carrying foam-topped surf boards. Cassidy watched them meet up with a hotel employee in the entryway who helped them stow their boards in a giant metal cage. The cage contained at least a hundred surfboards of all shapes and lengths. The employee, a petite woman in a blue polo shirt, her thick dark hair coiled tightly into a perfect bun, locked the cage. The two surfers slipped down the hallway.

"You surf?" the bartender asked her, swooping in with silverware and a napkin.

"Um," Cassidy said, turning away from the surfboard cage.

"We can set you up with a board, lessons...we even do tours," he added, placing a glass of water near her silverware.

By now she was so hungry she felt lightheaded, but the mention of tours got her attention. "Yes, I would like to find out about tours. Do you have a boat?" she asked.

The bartender nodded. "We run weekly trips to Witch's Rock and Ollie's Point, as well as day trips to local breaks like Avellanas, Nosara . . . "

"How big is the boat?" she asked.

The bartender looked puzzled. "Uh, normal sized?"

"*Lo siento*," she said, shaking her head. The conversation wasn't going where she wanted it to. "*Estoy buscando a alguien*," she said. *I'm looking for someone.*

"*A quién?*" he asked.

Cassidy pulled out her phone and swiped through her pictures. When was the last time her damaged family had been together? Christmas, two years ago? Or was it during her visit to Rebecca's after Gloria was born? Jeez, that was four years ago. Finally, she found a photo of Reeve. His brown hair hung loose—a little long, she always thought—and wearing that same goofy grin. Reeve's eyes were a brownish hazel that, when he was high, went from peaceful to downright terrifying. In this picture, he wasn't high, and his cheeks were filled out, which meant that he had probably been clean. Cassidy had forgotten how kind and normal he could look.

She flashed her screen at the bartender. He scrutinized the phone for an instant before saying, "Yeah. I've seen him around."

"When was the last time you saw him?" Cassidy asked.

The bartender crossed his arms and seemed to give the question some thought. "I guess it's been a while."

A stocky Tico in a red polo shirt brought her a giant plate of burrito, black beans, and rice. Cassidy's eyes nearly popped out of her head at the sight of so much food. She was used to eateries in her little town on the volcano where portion sizes were for normal humans.

"How long ago?" Cassidy asked.

The bartender wiped down a corner of the bar with a rag. "A few weeks?"

"Huh," she said, picking up her fork.

"*Otra cerveza?*" he asked, picking up her empty one.

Cassidy nodded.

When he returned, Cassidy was three bites into her burrito. "Did he work here?" she asked, forcing herself to slow down.

The bartender shook his head.

She took a sip of the ice-cold beer. "Or for someone with a boat?"

The bartender shrugged. "You might try Bruce Keolani. He runs surf tours out of Playas del Coco."

"Where's that?"

"North of here, about forty-five minutes."

Cassidy groaned inwardly.

"But Bruce usually comes around here in the mornings. Sometimes he picks up guests in Tamarindo."

"Even though you run surf tours too?"

He glanced at the TV. "Sometimes guests want to stay out longer, explore, that kind of thing. Bruce does that."

Cassidy nodded. The bartender assisted a waitress with a drink order, then left his post. She heard him picking up empty glasses and stacking plates. By the time he was back, Cassidy was stuffed.

"The kitchen is closing in a few minutes. Can I get you anything else?"

"You got rum?" she asked.

"Absolutely."

Cassidy scanned the shelves behind the bar, finding what she was looking for. "Then I'll take *Flor* on the rocks with an orange wedge."

"You got it."

Normally, she would celebrate the end of her fieldwork with a glass of Glenfiddich, but it didn't feel right, not in this surf depot. Nicaraguan rum was a close second and something she wouldn't easily find in the States. She paid her bill and arranged for a room for two nights, then wandered to a table outside where she could hear the waves.

Cassidy told herself that she would wait it out until morning when she could find this Bruce character, ask him if he knew anything about Reeve and where he had gone. Likely, Reeve just didn't show up for work one day, and would not have been seen since. She wondered if there was a girl involved. It was one of Reeve's patterns: stay straight for a while, then meet a gorgeous drug addict who was trying to get clean, but would fail and pull Reeve back into using. Refusing to experience it again, Cassidy had sworn to keep her distance. She shook her head once, vigorously, to clear the memories.

She sipped her rum, then bit down on her orange wedge, sucking the juice. She knew that if Reeve was indeed stuck in another one of these cycles, coming here to save him was a fool's errand.

Making her the fool.

THREE

A POUNDING on her door woke her sometime in the early morning. She had been dreaming that Arenal was erupting in bright red snakes of lava pouring down the mountainside. Héctor was pulling on her hand, telling her to run.

Cassidy slid her glasses onto her face and squinted at the clock: 6:07. She wrapped the cotton guest robe hanging in the closet around herself and hurried to the door, stepping over her gritty field clothes.

The knock sounded again as she yanked open the door. A man with thick, dark brown hair and playful brown eyes stood with one foot on the step and one on the walkway as if he were about to bound through her door. Black sunglasses were pushed to the top of his head, and his smooth skin—Japanese? Hawaiian, maybe?—was deeply tanned, with crow's feet surrounding his eyes. He could be twenty-eight or fifty.

He gave her a quick up-and-down, then tilted his head, as if not quite sure what to make of her. "You the one looking for Reeve?"

"Oh," Cassidy stammered. "Yes, that's me."

"I'm Bruce Keolani." They shook hands. Bruce's grip was firm, his thick callouses pressing into her palm. "Can you surf?"

"Yes," she said again.

"I got a tour going today—I'll take you along. Tell you what I know on the way."

Cassidy blinked. "Sure," she said.

"Be out front in five minutes. And bring your passport."

He stepped down from her doorstep.

"My passport?" she asked, but he was already out of sight.

Cassidy closed the door, fully awake now. She dove for her backpack and pulled out a bikini, board shorts, rash guard, and a clean T-shirt. After popping in her contacts, she grabbed her water bottle, sunscreen, hat, passport, a fistful of *colones*, rolled it all up in a guest towel and shuffled into her flip-flops. Before locking up her room, she took a last glance at the big, empty bed, wondering how many more nights she would spend in it.

Cassidy joined the group of surfers, three of them scruffy twenty-somethings, each yawning, and one couple, trim and expertly dressed —right down to the waterproof surf hats and zinc on their pale cheeks.

Bruce was on the roof of a mud-splattered jeep, cinching down surfboards.

"Hey *dormilona*," he called down to her. "I got you a seven-oh. You good with that?" he asked, leaning over the stack of boards.

Cassidy frowned at him. Sleepyhead, huh? She would ride any board, any length, but the last thing she needed was some pirate teasing her, no matter how handsome he was. And especially if it was about sleep—if he only knew how precious little she got.

"Sure," she grumbled.

Under normal circumstances, she would bring her own board, but not on a research trip. Dragging her fragile six-foot-two Al Merrick all the way to Arenal would have been a total pain in the neck. Rental boards were a dime a dozen down here. In between surf sessions, she planned to get some work by the pool and enjoy some downtime—something she hadn't prioritized in years—then go home to the rainy Northwest.

Although home wasn't really home anymore, with Pete no longer a part of it.

A wave of grief rose up inside her. She closed her eyes for a moment to push it away. When would these moments stop happening to her?

When she opened her eyes, the man and woman in matching sun hats were staring at her.

"*Vámonos,*" Bruce said, climbing down from the van's roof.

The surfers filed into the van; Cassidy sat in the front, next to the couple. Bruce did a U-turn on the quiet street and accelerated slowly out of town.

Bruce picked up a brown box from the front seat and handed it back to the woman sitting next to Cassidy. "Breakfast?" he asked the group. "I have coffee too," he added, reaching for another box packed tight with small disposable cups, each topped with a plastic lid.

The woman opened the box, took out a pastry, and passed the box to Cassidy, who chose a croissant. After passing the box to the seat behind them, Cassidy ate her flaky pastry and washed it down with the strong coffee. The surfers in the back row were waking up, their banter and hushed laughter filling the quiet space of the vehicle. The couple next to her said nothing, and Cassidy sat back and watched the fields and verdant jungle pass by, bracing herself against the deep ruts and holes in the road.

AFTER THE DRIVE, Bruce pulled the van to a stop in front of a grand but faded hotel with a wrap-around balcony. Cassidy slid the door open, and they all spilled out to the street.

"Go ahead inside," Bruce told them. "They're expecting you."

Cassidy fell in behind the group, but before continuing down the entryway steps, she heard giggles behind her. She turned back to see a handful of children gathering around Bruce.

"*Buenos días,*" he said to them with a twinkle in his eye. "*No hay escuela hoy?*"

They giggled, and the girl of the group, who was the tallest, said, "*No, tonto, no hasta después.*" There was a titter of giggles again.

"Tonto, huh?" he said to them, then quick as a flash, reached behind the littlest child's ear and brought out a coin. The children tittered again like a flock of tiny birds. Bruce climbed up to the jeep's roof, and the children dispersed.

Cassidy continued through the open-air hotel lobby and down a second set of stairs to two tables in the hotel's restaurant. She joined the couple at a table set on a covered balcony overlooking a broad, cocoa-brown beach. A waitress in a crisp, white button-down shirt and black skirt hovered at their table with a tray of coffee cups and a silver carafe. She placed the cups and coffee service on the table, and a minute later did the same for the three guys.

Bruce returned with a small stack of papers, which he distributed to them with a fistful of mismatched pens.

"These are so we can enter Santa Rosa National Park, where the waves are," he said, pointing to the page. "Just need to fill out the top," he added, and stepped to the other side of the restaurant where a lump was snoozing in a hammock hanging from the edge of the patio. Bruce tapped the lump, which stirred. A moment later, a slender, teenaged boy—a Tico—stood and stretched, then trotted barefoot out to the street.

Cassidy scanned the paper form and filled in the required information. The coffee was a step up from the cup she'd had in the van; she sat back and sipped it as she took in the scene. This must be Playas del Coco, meaning they were headed to Witch's Rock or Ollie's Point, two famous waves she had always wanted to surf.

Tall, brown cliffs closed in the sapphire-blue bay in front of the hotel to the North and South. The cliffs must block the swell because the bay was as flat as a lake.

Cassidy heard someone laugh and turned to see Bruce standing at the rear of the restaurant, sipping coffee from a gold-rimmed china cup with a person who she assumed, by the way he was dressed, was the hotel proprietor. Bruce slipped the man an envelope and disappeared.

The Tico boy made several trips back and forth from the street with the surfboards, carrying them through the hotel and down to the beach. He then rowed a dingy out to a medium-sized boat anchored to a faded orange buoy and climbed aboard.

Bruce returned to their tables, scooped up the paperwork, scanning each as he did so, and then tapped the pile against the table dramatically. "Drink up, mateys!" he said. "The surf waits for no one."

The group filed down to the beach and waded through soft, gushy sand to the idling boat. The Tico boy helped Cassidy aboard and gave her the "hang loose" sign flashed by surfers around the world. Cassidy gave him an appreciative smile in return. A thrill tingled low in her belly. Maybe searching for Reeve wasn't so bad if surfing the famous Witch's Rock was part of it.

As they motored slowly out of the bay, Bruce pulled down his sunglasses and topped his thick mop with a salt-stained trucker hat, pulling the bill low. The couple had seated themselves in front of the transom and were busy applying another coat of sunscreen, nibbling on gold-wrapped energy bars, and tightening the drawstrings of their nylon sun hats. The same three young males who had been chortling with each other since getting in the van had claimed the bow.

As a tour operator, Bruce likely knew a lot of people. This might be important in her search. Bruce could be more than a source of information. Maybe, he was someone she could bounce ideas off of. An ally.

"So, was Reeve one of your helpers?" Cassidy asked, seizing her chance to talk. In the van, she had thought to ride in the front, but the pastries and coffee had been in her way, and at the hotel in Playas del Coco, Bruce had been too busy.

She had imagined Reeve loading the boards in Tamarindo, or prepping the boat in Playas del Coco, or maybe even working as a mechanic. Reeve was handy with things like motors and could fix almost anything. But he was also not a legal resident and so would only be able to work jobs "under the table." If he worked at all.

"Yep," Bruce said, his eyes on the horizon. "Until one day he wasn't."

"What do you mean?"

"He ran my shuttle, helped with tours, like Augusto there." Bruce nodded towards the stern, where the Tico had his back to them, watching the shore recede. "I run tours up North every now and then. He worked a few of them." Bruce accelerated slightly as they cleared the edge of the bay.

In the distance, Cassidy saw miles and miles of ocean, with the brown and green land sloping into the sea ahead of them. Clearing the bay, they passed jumbles of rock and skimmed past cliffs that were getting sloshed by junky waves and currents.

"On my last trip, on the morning we were set to leave, he didn't show up."

"Like, he just ghosted you?"

He pursed his lips, as if thinking. "We had anchored overnight in San Juan del Sur," he said, then reached over to the cooler and pulled out an iced bottle of water, opened it, and took a sip. He must have noticed her confused look because he added, "Nicaragua."

Cassidy thought about this for a moment while trying to conjure up a map of the coastline. Nicaragua's southern border was only a short distance from their position, surely within a day's travel by boat.

"We'd hit epic Witch's and overnighted at Ollie's, surfed it at first light. He was doing some video for me, for the guests, but he got some waves, too," Bruce said, placing the water bottle in a cup holder attached to the nav station. "After that we surfed some select spots in southern Nica. I always overnight in San Juan. There's a great little bar right on the beach, some nightlife, good anchorage. The guests get a night in a four-star hotel, the whole deal. It's gorgeous. Anyways, the next morning, I get up first, make the coffee, you know, the ritual. But he doesn't come out of his cabin. Finally I knock—it was time to go pick up the guests—but he's not there."

"Did you go ashore? Ask around?" Cassidy asked. The boat was picking up speed, and the noise was making it hard to hear.

"Hell, yeah. I needed him." By now, Bruce was almost shouting over the engine noise. "No sign of him."

As they raced along steep gray-brown cliffs, the last vacation home disappeared, and soon there was only empty, barren wilderness. The boat zipped straight across the expansive, sapphire-blue sea, its surface peaky with a light chop.

Cassidy turned her face to the wind and closed her eyes, her mind spinning. She tried not to jump to conclusions. Reeve could have gone fishing that morning and drowned. Or had some kind of medical emergency that prevented him from getting back to the boat. But more likely, Reeve had gone ashore, blown his wad on drugs, and forgotten all about returning for work. He had left Bruce high and dry and looking foolish in front of clients. Bruce must have been furious. She knew how that felt. Reeve had ruined so many plans.

"Did he have a girlfriend?" she asked.

Bruce gave her a sideways glance. "I don't know if she was his girlfriend, but there was someone, yeah."

Cassidy took a deep breath and drank in the cool, fresh wind. So her hunch was correct: it was about a girl.

Her skin prickled with what felt like a discovery. It was a feeling she usually associated with her work—sometimes the data would reveal something surprising, or a creative door would open unexpectedly when she was writing.

"Do you know her name? Or where she might be?" Cassidy asked, watching Bruce's face.

Bruce squinted at her. "No. But I might know someone who does."

FOUR

"WHO?" Cassidy asked.

Bruce slowed the boat as they entered the bay, the square block of pale rock—Witch's Rock, or *Roca Bruja*—looming above them.

"I'll ask around, okay?" Bruce replied.

Cassidy told herself to be patient. Bruce had agreed to help, hadn't he? But she felt like Reeve was getting farther away from her with each passing minute.

The surfers on board were clambering to the gunnels to watch the waves pulse into the bay. A line of swell lifted the boat then surged on, breaking in a loud *boom*. The surfers in the bow started whistling, and hurried to get ready by donning rash guards and rubbing bars of wax across the decks of their boards.

The offshore winds were light, and the wave looked clean. Cassidy exhaled a deep breath, feeling the acute ache of Pete's absence. Another surf session without him. She slipped on her rash guard, picked up the loaner surfboard, and queued up to hop overboard.

Maybe it was the chilly river emptying into the ocean at Witch's

Rock, or maybe it was just her nerves, but she paddled away from the boat with goosebumps.

Cassidy joined the three guys and watched the first few waves to get her bearings. The couple, looking ready for war, joined the lineup as well. When a wave came her way, Cassidy spun for it. Anticipation tingled in her belly as she paddled two strokes and leapt to her feet. A light offshore wind brushed her face as she soared down the wave face.

The wave was lightning fast, arching up a few feet over her head. Before it could close out, she flew over the edge. It punched shut behind her in a roar.

"You're making good use of that board, I see," Bruce said, swimming over.

"Yes, thanks again." Cassidy would have preferred something a little shorter, but she appreciated his generosity. Even with the rub about being a sleepyhead, she was grateful that he had let her tag along.

A set wave swung wide, and Bruce started swimming furiously, his arms like windmills. Cassidy had to paddle outside to avoid getting trapped, but she watched Bruce drop in as she crested the lip. He extended his right arm, transforming his body into a long plank to skim the surface of the wave.

"You don't use a board, huh?" Cassidy asked when he swam back out. "Same as Reeve."

"Yeah," Bruce replied. "One of the things that impressed me about him."

"We surfed a lot as kids," Cassidy said when Bruce returned. Though Reeve always preferred just himself and the water. At the time, she had called him weird; it was just one more thing that Reeve did differently.

"Did he bodysurf on the Nicaragua trip?" she asked.

Bruce squinted, as if thinking. "Maybe? He was busy with filming. I remember him spending more time on the boat that trip. Editing, I guess."

The group continued trading waves until the wind kicked up, shearing the lips off the waves to blow shrapnel-like mist against her cheeks. It became difficult to see the drop while paddling into a wave because of the windborne spray.

Bruce rounded up the group, and one by one, they took their last waves and headed back to the boat, lined up like a row of ducklings. Augusto helped load everyone's boards, handing out waters or beers, and soon Bruce was pulling in the anchor.

Cassidy rinsed her face with fresh water from a jug on the stern, thinking about Reeve shirking good surf to edit footage of the guests. Taken at face value, it was a sign that Reeve had finally grown up. But his disappearance turned that conclusion on its head.

BUT BY THE time they returned to Coco Beach hours later, Cassidy still felt just as clueless about where Reeve was, or if he was okay.

A text message from Rebecca was waiting for her when they arrived:

Have you found out anything?

Cassidy tossed the phone on the bed and took a long shower, trying to use the time to organize her thoughts before replying,

He disappeared in Nicaragua.

What was he doing in Nicaragua?

He was working on a boat. He went ashore in San Juan del Sur and never came back.

Did you go there?

Cassidy frowned. *Go to Nicaragua?*

No, she typed.

There was a pause, and Cassidy was about to toss her phone back on the bed when it chirped.

Have you been to the police yet? They say they're looking into it but I don't think they are

Okay, I can go tomorrow. *Time for a drink*, she thought.

Rebecca replied with a "thumbs-up" emoji.

Cassidy took her laptop to the restaurant, where she ordered a plate of fried shrimp and beans. While she ate, she tidied up her inbox and then edited a paper she was collaborating on. Being a post-doc was sort of like having a two-year job interview; the university gave you money, and then everyone, including faculty at other universities that were hiring that year, sat back and watched how well you used it. The antidote to worrying about it was to publish like crazy.

So she pulled up her most important paper, the one detailing her work on Arenal. She was studying a type of seismic signal, called harmonic tremor because it could potentially help them predict the timing and scale of future eruptions. If she could establish this connection, it would be huge news, plus she'd have her pick of universities to start her career.

Her stomach tensed when she saw a note from Héctor. He had sent a short message saying that all six of their seismic stations were functioning.

"Yes!" she said out loud.

Because she wasn't scheduled to return to the volcano for another four months, this was excellent news. Though Héctor's note was professional, he did sign off with, "Be safe."

She was so lost in her work, taking breaks only to sneak bites of her food and sip her beer that when she was done, it was after ten o'clock, and her eyes felt gummy. In the corner above the bar, a basketball game was playing on the TV. The bartender she had spoken with the night before was leaning against the counter watching it, with a few other guests clustered nearby.

Cassidy paid her bill and slid out of her chair, feeling the soreness in her arms after the day of surfing and the stiffness in her butt from sitting so long. She approached the brightly lit bar and pulled up a stool. The bartender floated her way.

"So, are you Crazy Mike?" she asked, tucking one leg under the other.

"Nope," he said. "My Pop. He helped me build this place."

"Is he crazy?" she asked.

"He was, a little, but in a good way," he said with a tightness around his eyes.

"Oh," Cassidy said, chiding herself for intruding. "I didn't mean . . ."

He shrugged. "It's okay," he said, even though she could tell that it wasn't—something she understood intimately.

"I'm Mel," he said, and extended his hand.

Cassidy was grateful that he had changed the subject so gracefully. He shook Mel's hand. It was warm and firm. "Cassidy," she said.

"So, you've been glued to that screen of yours all night," he said, nodding at her vacated table. "Ready for a break?"

"As long as it's delicious."

His eyes flashed with a playful sparkle. "Hmm, don't tell me . . . ," he said, then closed his eyes and went into a pretend trance. "Mojito?" He opened his eyes.

"Sure," she said.

He gave her a look. "That wasn't what you were thinking, though, was it?"

"No, but a mojito sounds good," she replied with a shrug.

"Manhattan?" he asked.

"No."

He squinted again. "Margarita? I make the mix myself. Fresh lime. Raw honey."

She laughed, shook her head.

A look of enlightenment came over him. "Old fashioned."

Cassidy's gut took a dive, and her head felt like a bell that had just been rung. How could Mel have guessed such a thing? An image of Pete raising a birthday toast to her flooded her mind.

"No," she managed to say, her smile feeling tight. "Mojito, please."

Mel seemed to sense her mood shift, but covered it with a small bow. "As you wish," he said, and began making her drink with vigor.

"Thanks for connecting me with Bruce," she said when he returned with the drink, a pink umbrella speared through a lime wedge balanced on the lip.

"Sure," he said. "Good waves?"

She nodded. "Amazing. I'd always wanted to surf there."

He glanced at the TV where a player was shooting free throws—and made both of them. "Any info on your missing guy?"

A twinge of emotion tightened her gut. Why hadn't she admitted to Mel that Reeve was family? "He's, um, my stepbrother actually," she said, unable to look at him. Cassidy sipped from her drink. A rush of fresh lime and a tasty bite of sour woke up her taste buds. "I found out where he disappeared. He was working for Bruce on a tour that stopped in San Juan del Sur." Remembering the cool ocean breeze on her face while on the boat, she huffed out a breath of hot air.

Mel crossed his arms. "Nicaragua?"

Cassidy took another sip and licked the sugar off her lip.

"Do you think he could still be there?"

"I have no idea," Cassidy replied. Why would he get off the boat in Nicaragua? Weren't there enough drugs and girls and parties in Tamarindo?

"He hangs out with the surf guides sometimes. You might ask them if they know anything. They're usually surfing La Casita in the early morning."

"I don't have a board."

He raised an eyebrow, then pointed. "Take your pick," he said as she followed his finger to the board cage. "It's a fast little wave, fun on the kind of swell we've got running right now. Look for Macho and Eddie."

"Okay," Cassidy said. There was no harm in catching a few waves in the morning before her visit to the police station, right? Plus, she doubted the police were going to be able to tell her anything.

"How far away is San Juan del Sur?'" she asked.

Mel was back to watching the game, but crossed his arms and glanced back at her. "Depends on the border crossing. On a good day, it can take five hours, give or take. During a holiday or a busy weekend, it can take all day."

Cassidy thought about this.

"Want me to reserve a rental car for you?" he asked.

Cassidy was not ready to commit to such a thing. "How's the surf in Nicaragua?" she asked instead.

"There's some great breaks up there, but access is tricky. Most of the good waves are in front of fancy resorts, or the roads are crap. It's really better to go by boat."

On her way to her room, Cassidy stopped by the board cage and a petite woman let her in. She chose a rounded fish shape because it looked fun.

"Where's La Casita?" she asked the woman, whose name tag identified her as Aliana.

"Just north of the river," she said in perfect English. "There is a tiny, white house in front of the place where the wave breaks," she added.

Cassidy finished filling out her rental form, thanked Aliana, and, with her laptop tucked under one arm and her loaner board tucked under the other, shuffled down the walkway to her room.

Once inside, she placed the board on its side against the wall and her laptop in its case on the dresser. She thought she would send one last message to Rebecca about her plan to talk to Reeve's friends in the lineup. The steady supply of beers while she had worked, along with the nightcap afterwards, had the desired effect of making her feel a calm buzz she hoped would help her sleep. Where was her phone? She did a sweep of the room. Hadn't she left it on the bed? She checked the bathroom, then finally found it on the dresser.

Rebecca had already beaten her to a new message: There's great surfing near San Juan del Sur. I know you have the money.

Cassidy sighed and dropped onto the bed. When her father passed away, he had left most of his money to Quinn and herself; his wife Pamela didn't need it, and besides, the life insurance policy had covered all their debts. Her father had been an advertising executive, so the inheritance wasn't a small sum. It always made her feel weird whenever anyone found out about it. Most of it sat in a bank account and was managed by an investment firm her dad had set in place long ago. She wasn't rich, but she would certainly never go hungry. Most of the time, she tried to forget the money was there. Of course, Rebs made this impossible.

I'll think about it, she typed.

But as soon as she put the phone down, her annoyance at Rebecca faded, replaced by a feeling she couldn't quite place. Up until today, Cassidy had been going through the motions to confirm what she thought she knew about Reeve and what had happened to him—that he lapsed back into using and he was broke and dope sick under a palm tree somewhere. But the evidence wasn't matching up. Until the day he disappeared, Reeve had had a good job, a girlfriend, and as far as she could tell, had stayed clear of drugs.

Reeve's disappearance was too sudden. Too unlike Reeve to give it all up—even for a night of partying. His decline was usually much slower, with signs along the way that he was slipping back into old habits.

This could mean only one thing, and her blindness to it hit her hard: Reeve hadn't found trouble.

Trouble had found Reeve.

FIVE

THAT NIGHT, Cassidy had the same nightmare about Pete's crash. In it, she stood on a lonely curve of road, the fog floating on the wind past her cold face. On the pavement were the intersecting black skid marks, the single line from Pete's motorcycle, the doubles from the car he had tried to avoid hitting before his skid sent him off the road.

Cassidy had only been to the site once, with Quinn. She had made him take here there the day after Pete died. She needed to see it with her own eyes. To make sure it was real.

But it had likely been too much because the nightmare repeated regularly. In the dream, she followed the single tire track over the bank to the tree Pete had hit.

Cassidy woke with a gasp, clutching the sheets, her breaths fast inside her chest.

The dream ended this way every time. With her screaming for Pete as she stared at the empty row of trees, and her waking to a feeling of exhaustion. Of isolation and dread.

Hot tears leaked from her eyes. If only she had more answers, maybe her grief would soften. Why had Pete lost control that night? Why had he been driving so fast?

Cassidy breathed deeply and dipped into her usual visualization: walking with Quinn on a beautiful, white sandy beach. She imagined the crunch of the sand and the sound of the gentle waves, the smell of the sea and the honey-scented flowers growing on the trees at the edge of the shore. It took a moment, but the exercise helped her shift back to herself. Or what was left of her.

Knowing that further sleep would elude her, Cassidy got up and dressed for her surf session at La Casita and hopefully a meetup with the surf guides who knew Reeve.

The water was warmer than at Witch's Rock the day before, but still felt cool against her skin this early in the morning. A yellow blush was spreading across the horizon by the time she paddled out, first wading through the sandy shallows, then paddling hard for the outside. The fish-shaped surfboard felt a bit squirrelly under her, but she knew the two of them would bond soon enough.

She had never intended to be a surfer. Growing up in Boise, Idaho, she spent her summers outside riding her bike and playing in the creek, and her winters skiing. Back then her favorite activity was ballet, and she was on track to become quite good at it. But five years after her mother passed away, her father had reconnected with his high-school sweetheart and moved them to California.

Cassidy hadn't taken well to the move. She quit ballet after a year of classes in her new town—her southern California classmates were unbearably cruel, and the snooty ballet mistress had called her footwork "sloppy." Without ballet to anchor her, she drifted, and not in a positive way. By eighth grade, she had fallen in with the shady crowd that vandalized people's houses, smoked pot, and skipped school. But one of her boyfriends was a surfer and offered to teach her. In a way, she knew surfing had saved her, though it had made her even more of an outsider.

Reeve had been a surfer too, though he preferred using swim fins and his body to a board. The activity had bonded the two of them for a while, and Cassidy harbored some peaceful memories of their blended family at the beach, she and Reeve surfing while Quinn tried to pick up girls and Rebs worked on her tan while speed-reading romance novels. Most of the memories she had of Reeve weren't as favorable.

The waves at La Casita were shoulder-high and a little scruffy, but fast and fun, folding into little crash barrels that she tucked into after getting the feel of the board. She was starting to enjoy herself when three Ticos paddled out, bantering back and forth in their rapid Spanish. The sun had almost peeked over the hills behind them, and the shadow of the land was receding quickly.

The first Tico out gave her a nod, and then waited while she caught the next wave. *So, etiquette is alive and well in Costa Rica*, she thought. As she paddled back out, she watched the first Tico paddle for a wave and drop in, using the curve of water like a skate ramp, riding it up and down until it crumbled, and he flew over the back. She settled in to wait her turn next to the other two Ticos, who each gave her a nod. They traded waves in this way for a while until she and the first Tico, and his tangle of curly brown hair sparkling with seawater, were paddling back out side by side.

"Where you from?" he asked in adorably accented English, his smile open and friendly.

"Oregon," she replied.

"Ah," he said, though she wondered if he had any idea where that was. "How long you stay?" he asked.

Cassidy thought quickly. "A few days."

"*Bueno*. Tomorrow we have *olas más grandes*," he said, his deep brown eyes sparkling. "You should go to Playa Grande," he added. They reached the lineup and both sat up on their boards. The two other Ticos had taken waves, so it was just the two of them.

"I might be going to Nicaragua," she said to her surprise. Until that moment, she hadn't made a decision.

The Tico's eyes lit up. "*A dónde?*" he asked.

"I'm not sure where exactly," she said. "Do you know Bruce?"

"Cap-tain Kee-o!" he said in a husky-sounding chant, then paddled off for a wave and disappeared. The other two returned to the lineup, and Cassidy noticed a handful of other surfers getting ready to paddle out.

"Here come the crowds," one of the Ticos nearby muttered when she turned back to the horizon.

"You guys work at the camp?" she asked.

"Yes. I am surf guide," he said with a hint of pride. "Rico is instructor," he added, tilting his head toward his friend.

"And him?" Cassidy asked, nodding toward the Tico she had talked to first.

"He is surf guide too," he answered. "You stay at the camp?"

"Yes," she replied.

He pointed to himself and said, "Macho." Then he pointed to the surfer to his left, who was paddling into a wave. "Rico." Then the third Tico paddled up. "Eddie."

"*Mucho gusto*," Cassidy said with a nod. "Cassidy."

"*Mucho gusto*," Eddie and Macho chorused.

With a jolt, she realized that she'd been surfing side by side with the people she had hoped to find.

"You take tours today, Cassi-dee?" Macho asked before she could bring up Reeve. "I think we go to Avellanas. Is beautiful beach. Muchas olas." Macho then spun for a wave and started paddling.

The idea of spending the day trading waves with Macho sounded tempting, but she needed to get to the police station.

"*Adios*, Cassi-dee," Eddie said, then stroked into a wave and was gone.

"Wait," she called, but it was too late. Quickly, she stroked into a wave and surfed it, trying to pick out Macho in the group of surfers collecting on the shore. Her wave collapsed with a thud behind her and she dropped to her belly to ride the whitewash in.

"Do you guys know Reeve Bennington?" she asked when she reached the threesome.

Macho paused the coiling of his leash. He glanced at Eddie and Macho, then back at her.

"*Sí*," Macho answered.

"We haven't seen him in a while," Eddie added.

"I know. I'm trying to get in touch with him."

Eddie eyed her curiously. "Is he okay?"

A tendril of guilt tickled her insides. "I don't know. He normally checks in with Rebecca, his sister, but he hasn't, so I'm here."

"*Vámonos*," Macho said. "We can walk back together," he said. Eddie and Rico were already walking toward the river, deep in conversation. Something about a surfboard.

"So his sister ask you to come?"

Cassidy nodded.

"Why she not come? Is beautiful, yes?" He gestured with his free arm at the jungle and the sunrise.

"She has too many children," Cassidy replied, then realized how that sounded. "I mean, her kids are little. And her husband travels a lot."

"Is he your friend?"

"No. Stepbrother. We grew up . . . for a time . . . together."

"Ah." This information seemed to satisfy Macho.

"So, can you tell me about him?" Cassidy asked.

"He surfed sometimes," Macho began. "Like this, here. I see him out sometimes. At the club. On the beach. Is party town, right?" he said, a little sheepishly.

"What club?"

"They have music. Reggae, you know, for dancing. It is up past the circle." He looked at her to see if she was following him. Cassidy nodded, figuring that the circle was where the road forked away from the beach.

"Was he doing drugs?"

Macho looked at her in surprise.

"Sorry, it's just . . . I'm used to it. Reeve has had problems in the past," she said, trying to keep her tone light.

"It is not my place to say," Macho said.

Now it was Cassidy's turn to be surprised.

"Smoke a little motta, have few beers, sure, I see this. But this is everybody," he conceded.

"But no needles, pills?"

A look of extreme discomfort came over his face. "I would not know this. We only surf together sometimes."

"I'm sorry. I just can't help but think he got into some kind of trouble. He got off the boat in San Juan del Sur and never came back. Maybe he was using again. Maybe he was on the run, or maybe he just got pulled back into that life."

"He go to San Juan?" Macho asked.

"He was working a trip with Bruce," Cassidy answered. "You call him Captain Keo, right?"

Macho nodded. "Yes, I remember this. Reeve helps out. Fix things. Does video for the guests." He sighed. "He's a good guy. Good surfer too. One time he fixed my bike. I was going to be late to work, and he's just coming home from the night, and he says, 'let me look at it.' Five minutes later and boom, it's fixed. Freaking genius, that guy."

They had reached the river and began to wade in, then went prone and paddled across, the current sweeping them downstream at an angle. On the other side, Eddie and Rico were waiting for them.

"Did he hang out with anyone? Apparently, there was a girl. Do you know who she is?"

All three shook their heads.

"Meet us tonight," Macho said, eyeing the others, including them. "We can show you where he lives."

SIX

CASSIDY RETURNED her board to the cage, showered, and dressed carefully in her least grubby clothes. Not a small feat, given that she had not intended to impress anyone on this trip, which had transitioned from fieldwork to surfing. After a cup of coffee and eggs from the restaurant, she asked directions to the police station from the hostess.

The breeze coming from the mountains tasted fresh, faintly of blossoms. On her walk, the gentle hum of insects kept her company.

She followed the dirt street to the edge of town and found the low, white building with two blue motorcycles parked outside and a Costa Rican flag tacked to the exterior wall. If not for the barred windows, she could have mistaken it for a community center.

She entered the open doorway, where a man with a round face wearing a blue uniform sat talking on the phone behind a scuffed metal desk. He grunted a sign-off and hung up.

"*Puedo ayudarla?*" he asked with an inquisitive gaze.

Cassidy bit her lip. "*Una persona desaparecida.*"

The man's eyebrow rose.

There was no chair in the room. Beyond the entryway office

space was a larger room with a table, folding metal chairs, and a medium refrigerator, stained brown at the edges and decorated with a handful of stickers from surf companies and energy drinks.

"*Tu marido?*" the officer asked.

A painful jolt shot down her spine. *Husband.* Cassidy shuffled her feet to keep her knees from wobbling.

"No," she managed. "*Mi hermano.*"

Spanish had no word for "stepbrother" so "brother" would have to do.

The officer raised an eyebrow. "*Cuándo?*"

"*Tres semanas.*"

The man calmly pulled out a form from a slot mounted on the wall and handed it to her. While she filled out the form, the man left the room, his aggressive footsteps vibrating the floor.

Describing the events leading up to Reeve's disappearance in Spanish was a challenge, but she did her best. Once finished, she peeked into the bigger room. An officer stood in the doorway of an office at the end of a short hallway, waving her to enter.

The officer, a middle-aged man with generous love handles and a thin, frowning mouth took her form and gestured toward a yellow velour chair pushed against the wall. Cassidy obeyed, though it felt awkward to be so far from the desk.

The man settled into the red vinyl folding chair and began reading her form, underlining specific phrases and muttering to himself. Cassidy took in the room with its dingy, scuffed walls, the wavy orange-brown water stain snaking down the seam, and the uneven blinds on the window.

Something shifted in the officer's eyes. He paused, as if making a connection. Frowning, he licked a finger and began leafing through his stack of papers, then pulled one out and placed it next to her form, tapping his pen back and forth on certain details as he scanned.

"Is this your missing person?" he asked in heavily accented English, offering her the paper.

It was Rebecca's report. So her information *had* gotten through after all.

"*Sí*," Cassidy replied.

With a grimace, the officer placed both papers on the pile. He sat back, his arms crossed over his chest. "You can try asking at OIJ. But because he was last seen in Nicaragua, there is not much we can do."

A heavy feeling dropped through her. Another dead end. "What's the OIJ?"

"*Organismo de Investigación Judicial*. It is for more serious crimes," he replied.

Cassidy's stomach clenched. *More serious.* Him disappearing wasn't serious enough? "Was he ever arrested in Tamarindo?" she asked.

With a sigh, the officer stood and walked to the filing cabinet, where he slid open a drawer and thumbed down the files. He plucked one, his eyebrows peaked, and scanned the contents.

"He assaulted a taxi driver two months ago."

Cassidy grabbed the sides of her chair to steady herself. This was exactly what she had feared. Reeve wasn't normally violent—unless he was using.

"Was the taxi driver okay?"

The officer glanced back at the file. "I do not know."

Cassidy sat back and tried to think. "Does it say why he was assaulting a taxi driver?"

The cop shook his head. "Ask the OIJ. They do the investigating."

"Where is the OIJ?"

"In Santa Cruz."

The man opened a drawer in his desk and slid out a single sheet of paper. It was a printed map with directions, including bus routes.

Though this was the natural place for her to make her leave, she had one more line of questioning. "Would your files show any record of an overdose?"

The officer shook his head. "Only if we respond, such as for violence."

Cassidy gave him a searching look.

"He is not in our files except for the assault. But you could inquire at the clinic. They know more than we do. Many times a person is brought in without us being notified."

Cassidy thought about this. "Does Tamarindo have a lot of overdoses?"

The officer's eyes darkened. "It is a growing problem."

She crossed her arms. *Now we're getting somewhere.*

"How many?"

"Two this month already," the man said, his eyes troubled.

"And you're sure Reeve wasn't one of them?"

The man shook his head. "One was a tourist. One was a young female."

Cassidy grimaced. *How young?* she wanted to ask.

"Prostitution is legal in Costa Rica," he added, as if this explained it. "I think you will find more answers at the OIJ," the man said, and stood.

Cassidy stood and thanked the officer, then walked back through the entryway, nodding to the officer stationed there as she passed before stepping back onto the street.

THE HOT BUS ride to Santa Cruz did not improve Cassidy's mood, and by the time she stomped up the steps to the OIJ, her shirt was wet with sweat, her throat was dry, and a blister was starting to grow its ugly head between two of her toes.

A whoosh of air-conditioned breeze blasted her face as she entered a modern building with marble floors and high ceilings. She placed her request to speak with an officer and was told to sit and wait, which she did in an upholstered chair next to a vending machine displaying typical junk food. A row of posters on the wall warned against the dangers of drug use, another blared a hotline for illegal industrial dumping, and another displayed a halting image of a young girl sitting on a bed in a sparse room. Beneath it were the words: *Dejen de vender a nuestros hijos.* Stop selling our children.

A man in plain clothes called her name.

"Detective José Miranda," the man said, then indicated for her to follow him. They walked to a brightly lit office furnished with wooden chairs and a gray metal desk with a computer resting on the far corner.

"You say you have lost your brother," Detective Miranda said — thankfully in English.

"My stepbrother," she corrected. "He hasn't checked in for a few weeks. His sister is worried that something has happened to him."

"Mmm," Detective Miranda replied.

He was tapping a key on his computer. "And you filed your report with the local police?"

"Yes," she said. "Though they told me that because he was last seen in Nicaragua, there is not much they can do. I was hoping you could tell me something different."

He gave her a sympathetic look. "I'm afraid your information is correct."

"What if he was running from something? He attacked a taxi driver. What if someone was coming after him, to get back at him, or something?" Cassidy knew this sounded far-fetched, but Reeve could be unpredictable. "There've been murders in Costa Rica, for drug trafficking and smuggling. Could he have been involved in something illegal like that?"

"The report for his assault is here, but it looks like he was fined and then released. I see no drug-related charges."

"How about heroin overdoses? The local police agreed it's a problem."

The detective's eyes flashed. "Heroin is a problem everywhere. Tamarindo is not unique."

"But do your records show if the assault was related to heroin sales, or activity, or if the victim or Reeve ever overdosed?"

Detective Miranda shook his head.

Cassidy switched tracks. "Did Reeve pay his fine?"

"Yes," Detective Miranda said after a glance at the screen.

"Could he have fled to Nicaragua because he was being chased by someone?"

"It's possible," the detective said, though not very convincingly.

Cassidy sat back and sighed. This was going nowhere. "Should I go to Nicaragua?"

The detective shot her a look of scrutiny. "I cannot answer that for you."

"Well, are you going to look into it, at least? He was living in Tamarindo before he disappeared. He's a U.S. citizen."

"You could try the U.S. Embassy in San José."

"No," Cassidy growled, as her head began to throb. She had spent enough time on this wild goose chase.

"How do you know foul play is a factor?" the detective asked, shifting in his chair. "Sometimes people want to disappear."

The poster of the young girl in the hotel room flashed into her mind. "Could he have been kidnapped?"

"Yes," the detective said slowly. "But from what you say, he came ashore in San Juan del Sur of his own free will and did not come back."

"So he could have been kidnapped in San Juan."

"Yes."

They both sat in silence for a moment. Cassidy knew that if some kind of crime or kidnapping had occurred in Nicaragua more than two weeks ago, Reeve was probably . . . she couldn't finish the thought. He had called her for help. And she had ignored him, too consumed with her own pain to answer the phone. A sense of doom pulled at her already raw emotions. If Reeve was dead, how would she break it to his family?

After a tense goodbye, Cassidy slipped outside the office, the bright sun making her squint. The lowering sun had heated the air to a sultry inferno that made her head dizzy and set her legs on fire.

Somehow, she made it to the bus stop, boarded the correct bus, and collapsed into the nearest empty seat.

The ache in her chest that had begun to throb in the detective's office now expanded to her shoulders, thighs...even her ears were ringing. Everything was too bright, too loud. She curled into a ball, tucking her head down, and tried to close it all out.

It was worse than she thought. Reeve was using again, getting into fights. Was it only a matter of time before he killed someone?

Maybe it's time to stop searching.

SEVEN

BACK AT CRAZY MIKE'S, Happy Hour was in full swing, making the bar too noisy to work. Out at the beach, the softly breaking waves were lit by a lime-green glow, with surfers dotting the lineup. It wasn't a hard choice.

After a quick change, she borrowed a longboard and paddled it outside the breakers. Shading her eyes against the low-lying sun as she sat waiting, she took in the other surfers in the lineup, recognizing Macho and Eddie. Behind her, the distant purple-black mountains presided over the landscape like a royal court.

A wave came her way, and she swung the big board around, paddled a few strokes, and dropped in. Down the line, another surfer yelled, "Party wave!"

Cassidy released her frustration from her dead-end day chasing Reeve and laughed. While paddling back out, Macho came alongside her.

"*Buenos tardes,*" he said with a bright grin, his squiggly curls dappled with tiny drops of seawater shining like golden beads in the low sun.

"*Tardes,*" Cassidy echoed—keeping it short on purpose in case he started talking about Reeve or the visit to his apartment he had promised. She wasn't sure she wanted to see it now, after what she'd learned today.

At the lineup, she twisted her hair into a messy bun and secured it with an elastic she pulled off her wrist.

Eddie and Macho paddled out and joined them.

"Yo, Cassi-dee!" Eddie said in greeting. "You going out with us tonight?" He gave her a little splash. "Hotel Simpatico is throwing a pool party."

"You must come!" Macho said, and Rico joined in. "They have diving contests. And jello shots!"

Cassidy took a wave, then watched Macho and Eddie try to tandem surf. Then Rico took off and did a headstand. Soon, she was laughing away her doomsday mood.

The sun was approaching the horizon, coating the water with a coppery sheen, when a small power boat with a simple canopy approached from the south. Lining the gunnels were the easily identifiable silhouettes of surfers, with Bruce at the helm.

Recognizing him brought on a strange feeling she couldn't place. Anxiety? Anticipation? He idled the boat a hundred yards outside of the lineup as the surfers grabbed their boards and hopped over the side.

"Cap-tain Keo-O!" Macho and Eddie chanted.

Bruce replied with a shaka, his white grin visible in the low light.

When he saw her watching, he motioned her over.

"You going to get into tandem surfing next?" he teased, nodding at Eddie and Rico dropping into a wave together, with Rico lifting Eddie onto his shoulders.

"Hardly," she said with a grin. "Did you get any information on Reeve's girlfriend?"

"No, sorry. My source is in the wind," he replied, his expression turning serious. "What about you? Any new leads?"

She sighed, and rubbed the deck of her board with a scoop of seawater. "Apparently he attacked a taxi driver."

Bruce frowned. "Where was this?"

"Somewhere in Tamarindo." She squinted at the lowering sun. "At night. About two months ago."

"Huh," he said, pursing his lips.

"He paid a fine, and that was it."

Bruce shrugged. "Guy gets drunk, taxi driver tries to cheat the guy . . . it can get ugly, I suppose."

An idea came to her. "Hey, when's your next Nicaragua trip?"

He gave her a curious look. "Tomorrow, actually. I've got a five-day tour with some repeat clients. "Why?"

"I thought about going there."

Bruce raised an eyebrow. "You want to tag along?"

Her stomach fluttered. "Are you serious?"

His eyes widened as he scrutinized her. "I'd have to clear it with the group, of course, and I'm not sure . . . "

"Forget it," Cassidy interrupted. "I don't want it to be weird."

"You can take a bus to San Juan, you know," Bruce said.

"I know. I'm just not stoked for an eight-hour trip." If she was the kind of person who could read on busses, it might not be so bad. She could kill two birds with one stone—tackle some more editing, get caught up on some reading. But as a kid, she had thrown up in cars so many times while trying to escape into a book that her father stashed airline sickness bags for her in the backseat. These days, she used vehicle time to catch up on sleep, but she certainly wouldn't need eight hours of it. And then she would have no idea where to go in San Juan. She needed Bruce to show her.

"Why don't I ask the group? No harm if they say no," Bruce said with a shrug.

"I can pay my way, of course." *You have the money,* Rebecca's voice reminded her.

Bruce nodded. "I can let you know tonight."

Cassidy watched Bruce cruise out of the bay and disappear into the shimmering sun.

Was it a waste of time to continue chasing Reeve?

She was due back in Eugene in just a few days. Maybe now was the time to pull the plug.

But Reeve had called her for a reason.

Finally, she took her final wave in, a black wall she navigated by sound because it was so dark. On the shore, while wrapping up her leash, music and the din of conversation from the crowded bar drifted over the sand.

Macho shook his wild curls dry, and Eddie stepped over, his normally playful eyes serious.

"Meet us outside the bar in ten," he said. "We'll show you Reeve's apartment."

AFTER A QUICK RINSE, Cassidy threw on a pair of cutoff shorts and a t-shirt, then hurried to the street.

Macho, Eddie, and Rico stood waiting, each with a mountain bike.

"*Vámonos*," Macho said, motioning for her to get on his handlebars.

"What?" she asked, looking at him in alarm. A bead of sweat trickled down her temple. "If I sit up there, you won't be able to see!"

He made a noise like a punctured tire. "My brother and I do it all the time," he said and pointed to the nubs of metal poking out from each side of the front wheel's hub. "Your feet go here. Eet no problem."

Cassidy eyed the bike, a late-model single speed with bare handlebars and splattered with many layers of dried mud. Accepting her fate with a sigh, with Macho's help, she climbed on.

Then Macho was off, and Cassidy had a front-row seat as they sped down the muddy street.

They raced down the dark main road, passing pedestrians, dodging cars with music blaring. Cassidy gripped the handlebars and tried to keep her feet from slipping off the tiny metal nubs on the wheel. After catching up with Eddie and Rico, the three egged each other on with insults and their infectious laughter. They rode past the circle and up a hill. The fancy hotels and restaurants transitioned to smaller and smaller buildings. Most had tin roofs and open doorways. Even though there was reggae music thumping from somewhere, there was little activity, as if the buildings themselves were holding their breath.

Macho stopped in front of a concrete apartment building. Cassidy slid off the handlebars. The Ticos stashed their bikes alongside the entryway, tucked between the walkway and the overgrown patch of jungle occupying the neighboring lot. Cassidy followed them up a narrow stairway to the second floor.

The concrete walls were scuffed with gray marks. One section was covered in watery tan splatters, as if someone with bad aim had thrown out their dirty dishwater. A woman's voice shouted from one of the units above them. There was also the faint sound of singing coming from farther off down the street.

"*Cúal?*" Eddie asked Macho.

Macho walked slowly, glancing from one side of the hall to the other, until he stopped in front of the door at the end.

Cassidy paused. It looked like an ordinary door to an ordinary—if slightly seedy—apartment, like many others she imagined Reeve living in over the years. When he wasn't on the street or in jail. What should she do? Knock?

The Ticos didn't seem to know what to do either, and started chattering, their nervous giggles filling the cramped hallway.

Cassidy knew Reeve was not in the room behind the door.

She took a deep breath and knocked, soft at first. Then louder.

Nothing happened. She pounded again. What would she tell Rebecca? Harder now. She tried the doorknob, and it wiggled, then clanked in an odd-sounding way. She pulled her hand back, spooked. On closer inspection she realized that the locking mechanism was broken—the whole knob practically fell apart in her hands. She gave the door a little push, and it popped open.

Macho's eyes were wide. Eddie and Rico stopped talking and the hall was silent again.

The apartment inside was dark. Should she go in? Something told her not to. She looked at Macho.

He shrugged. "Maybe people know he leave. They break in."

After a deep breath, Cassidy stepped inside.

EIGHT

MACHO PULLED the string dangling from the ceiling, and a dim glow from the bare overhead bulb illuminated the tiny studio.

Cassidy sucked in a gasp. The place was a mess—the bed, a single mattress on the floor, had been upended; the drawers in a dilapidated dresser had been pulled out and emptied. One had probably been thrown against a wall because it was in pieces in the corner, the cheap plywood splinters poking out of the broken edges like needles. Some clothes were on the floor, presumably from the dresser drawers when they were dumped: surf brand T-shirts and a few pairs of board shorts, boxer shorts, a threadbare yellow fleece that he probably never wore in such a climate, and a pair of rubber flip-flops, one of them with a broken strap.

Macho whistled.

Cassidy blinked at the destruction, fighting the unease building in her gut. While Reeve could be destructive, whatever happened here wasn't caused by a surf bum on a bender.

The bathroom, a single toilet with no seat and a tiny sink attached to the wall, was empty. No toothbrush or shaving cream, towel. Empty.

"Are you sure this is Reeve's place?" she asked Macho.

Macho looked uneasy. "Sí," he said.

Cassidy looked again at the room. A poster on the wall for a reggae band she had never heard of was ripped down the middle, exposing a hole in the wall's plaster. Had Reeve put up the poster to cover the hole? Or had the raiders made the hole when they ripped the poster down? What had they been after, anyway? Reeve was not a rich person. Had he kept expensive electronics in here? He was doing video for Bruce's guests. Maybe he owned some of the equipment himself. Had it been stolen? There was a yellowed and dinged up shortboard in the corner, surprisingly in one piece. She knew it was worthless—it likely didn't even float.

"Macho," Rico moaned. "*Vámonos,*" he added with a nod towards the exit. Macho shot him a stern gaze. Eddie looked subdued. He shook his head at Cassidy, and then slunk outside. Rico followed, and she could hear the two of them whispering outside.

"Happens sometimes," Macho said, indicating the mess. "*Lo siento.*"

She stepped forward to the dresser. One drawer was still attached. Unable to stop herself, she slid it open, hoping for what, she didn't know. But it was empty. She looked around the room again.

"He ees not here," Macho said softly.

In a daze, Cassidy nodded. They stepped back into the hallway and closed the broken door.

Eddie and Rico were already hurrying down the hallway, their low voices echoing off the dingy walls. From the stairway, a man entered the hall, leading a young woman by the hand. They slipped by Eddie and Rico. The young woman looked more like a girl, with thick, long hair braided to the side and a flower tucked behind her ear. Her skin was golden brown and flawless, and she was wearing a short skirt and a halter-top. The man was Caucasian, late twenties, with a buzz cut and a stubbly face, like he was growing a beard, but who would grow a beard in this heat? He wore long, loose basketball shorts and a wrinkled short-sleeved button-down shirt adorned with palm trees. Cassidy watched this couple approach with a growing sense of unease. Macho too, seemed tense.

The man gave her only a rushed glance when he passed, keeping his head low. The young woman did not look at them, but simply followed behind, her eyes on the ground. Cassidy watched them walk to the apartment across from Reeve's, then the man pulled out a key and unlocked the door. They were about to step inside when Cassidy cried "wait!" but it came out like a croak, and the door closed.

Cassidy took a step towards it, but Macho hissed a warning.

"What's wrong?" she asked, confused.

"Mebee come back tomorrow," he said, his eyes tight.

Cassidy glanced at the closed door, then back at Macho. "He lives across from Reeve. What if he knows what happened in there?"

Macho sighed. "I wait on the street."

Cassidy gathered her courage and closed the distance to the door. She knocked. Waited. When no sounds came from behind the door, she knocked again.

A groan came from inside the apartment. The door popped open to reveal the scruffy-faced man. He was now shirtless. "What?" the man growled, his eyes angry.

"Um, I'm looking for Reeve," she said, looking over her shoulder at his broken door. "Do you know him?"

The man's lips tightened. "Yeah, he's gone though."

"I kind of got that," Cassidy said, fighting her impatience. "Any idea what happened in there?"

"You his girlfriend?"

Cassidy shook her head. "No. My stepbrother."

The man scrubbed his whiskery cheek with his fingertips, and glanced to the inside of the apartment. "I'm kinda busy right now."

"I won't keep you much longer," Cassidy said. "Was he in trouble?"

"Ha!" the man said with an amused cackle, his eyes bugging out. "Not more than the rest of us."

"Was he into drugs?"

The man's smile faded. "Not my business."

"Did you guys ever talk? Did he tell you why he left?"

"No," the man said. "We partied sometimes, you know, with the girls, but he didn't exactly share our future plans."

Sensing the man's impatience, she tried to think fast. "Did he have any friends that you know of? Or a girlfriend?"

The man looked thoughtful for a moment, as if sizing her up.

"Please," Cassidy begged.

The man shuffled his feet and sighed. "All right. There was one girl. He did get kinda crazy about her, you know?" He shook his head.

"Do you know her name?" Cassidy pressed.

The man closed his eyes, as if concentrating. "Jade," he said finally, looking as surprised as she was. "Now if you'll excuse me," he said, and closed the door.

Cassidy walked back to the bikes on jittery legs. It seemed as if the humidity had cranked up several notches since she'd entered the building, and she stepped outside feeling drenched.

The boys were leaning against the wall, talking in low tones.

Macho pushed off the wall. "*Listo?*" he asked, his eyes hopeful.

"The girl in the hallway," Cassidy said, rethinking the exchange, starting with the man's walk down the hallway to the *I'm a little busy right now* comment. "Is she . . . "

"*Chica,*" Eddie said, his normally cheerful face grave.

Cassidy frowned. Clearly, there was a different translation, because *girl* would not get this kind of response. "A prostitute?"

"Legal in Costa Rica," Rico said with a shrug.

The local police officer had used the same phrase earlier that day, as if it explained everything.

"But she was so young," Cassidy replied, disgusted at the thought of what she had interrupted.

Macho gazed across the street to where a man stood in the shadows scrolling his phone and smoking a cigarette.

"Sometimes there are girls who don't have a choice," he said.

"Their family sells them to people who do this. Or they are kidnapped and forced into it." He glanced back at her.

Cassidy shuddered again. She remembered the anti-trafficking poster at the police station and the many news stories she had read about this very problem, happening all over the world. Pete had even chased a story about it once.

"I think I'll walk back," she said to Macho who was waiting astride his bike.

"You sure?" Macho replied, his expression wary.

Did he glance at the man in the shadows, or had she imagined it? Cassidy nodded.

"Come on, Cassi-dee," Eddie said, pulling her into a little dance. His youthful muscles pressed against her as they moved. "Our work here is done. Now we party."

Rico whistled.

Cassidy broke away with a laugh. "Another time, *amigos.*"

THE STREETS FELT MUCH MORE unfriendly without her escorts, but Cassidy almost welcomed it, daring shadows to jump out at her so she could unleash her growing anguish. The many pieces of Reeve's story rattled around in her brain. The police station and the detective. The apartment. The neighbor with his *chica.* She wished she could push a button to make the images fall into a hole and never return.

Cassidy bought a flask of rum from a shop at the edge of town and meandered through a gap in the shops to the beach. A steady breeze blew from the land, lifting strands of her hair to tickle her hot face. The sound of the waves combing the shoreline blocked out the noise and music of the town.

She started walking, away from it all, sipping from the flask when she felt like it. Walking on the beach while watching the moon glow on the water and enjoying the rum's smooth bite had the calming effect she was looking for, and soon she was back at the beach fronting Crazy Mike's. She sat in the sand and tried to piece together what she knew.

The conversation with the police officer felt like it was full of holes. Why hadn't she asked for more information about the over-doses, or the name of the taxi driver whom Reeve had assaulted, or more about the clinic where Reeve may have been taken? Then there was the neighbor and Reeve's girl, Jade. Was she a *chica*? Did prosti-tutes have boyfriends? That seemed weird—but she supposed it was possible. Prostitution was a job like any other, so that didn't mean a girl couldn't be in a relationship. The big question was if Reeve had stolen something and then run away, and someone had come looking for it. What would he have stolen? Drugs? Money? Or was the break-in just a run-of-the-mill burglary in an abandoned flat?

By the time she left the beach, it was well past midnight. She wondered if Mel was still at the bar. Would he know about the *chica* named Jade? Walking back from the beach, she missed the path that took her to the restaurant and found herself in the alley between the hotel and jungle buzzing with insect activity.

She stood trying to decide if she should continue out to the street and then loop back to Crazy Mike's front entrance, or retrace her steps and go in through the bar, when a figure emerged from a path cutting through the jungle.

It was a woman, smoothing down her skirt before turning toward the street.

Cassidy hurried after her, pulled forward by reckless curiosity. What had Reeve's neighbor said? *We sometimes party with the girls.* Had he meant *chicas*?

Could this woman know Jade?

NINE

THE WOMAN TURNED AROUND SHARPLY to face Cassidy.

"You following me?" she asked in Caribbean-accented English while looking Cassidy up and down.

"No, um, I'm looking for someone," Cassidy blurted.

The woman spun and began walking again.

Cassidy switched to Spanish. "*Mi hermano. Él ha desaparecido.*"

The woman paused, then turned back. "You got money?"

"Yes," Cassidy said, digging into her pockets for what she had stashed there—the equivalent of about twenty dollars in *colones*.

The woman's black eyes smoldered as she sauntered back and took the money, stuffing it into her bustier-like top.

"Who is your brother?" she asked, crossing her arms.

"His name is Reeve," Cassidy replied. "He disappeared two weeks ago. He was living in Tamarindo." She pulled up the picture of him on her phone and flashed it at the woman.

The woman took a one-second glance at the photo. She shrugged.

"He might have hired . . . er . . . " Was *chica* a slur? She switched tracks. "His apartment has been broken into—I was just there—and everything is torn up."

One of her penciled eyebrows arched. "Mebee he make bad enemies."

"He had a *chica* girlfriend, Jade," Cassidy said, watching the woman's face for a sign that the word offended her.

"I work alone," the woman said with a hint of pride. "I don't know this Jade." Then she spun and sauntered off into the night.

Cassidy stood watching, feeling helpless. If the *chicas* were independent, which meant no pimp, no brothel, how did they find clients? At the bars and clubs? Referrals?

Heavy dread sunk through her. If Jade was linked to finding Reeve, then Reeve would never be found. Cassidy wasn't an investigator. She didn't know how to slip into the underbelly of society, hunting for people like Jade, searching for clues in Reeve's trashed apartment. The feeling of doom from earlier that it was time to give up returned.

At Crazy Mike's, the lights were low and the candles on the tables flickered softly. Only a few tables were still occupied. A couple was finishing their drinks, a group of rowdy surfers were downing pints, and a big table of gap-year-age kids were paying their bill.

Mel was pouring beers from the tap when Cassidy slid onto a stool. He was wearing a black linen shirt and had tucked a pencil behind his ear. "*Buenas tardes, muñeca*," he said, his serene eyes flicking her way as he filled a pint from the tap.

The easy way he'd let the endearment roll off his tongue sparked a tiny flame inside her. "*Buenas tardes*," she replied.

Mel served up a tray of beers to a waitress. "Tell them last call," he told her, who nodded and left with the tray.

"*Una bebida?*" Mel asked her, his hands on his hips.

Cassidy shook her head. The motion caused her head to swim. She took a deep breath. "No, I . . . "

Mel gave her a concerned glance. "Rough day?"

Cassidy swallowed. The day had started with such promise, the surf session and meeting the playful Ticos lifting her sprits. Reeve had been helpful to them the way Cassidy knew he could be, and was, when he wasn't high. But then the disinterested police officers with their lack of compassion or any sort of emotion she could lean on...then the chicas, that trashed apartment...

This search was starting to take a toll on her. After today, she would have a whole new crop of images for her nightmares. This would be a good place to let it all go. To spend the rest of her time surfing and trying to forget about Reeve's plight.

Could she really walk away from Reeve now, though?

Mel placed a drink in front of her. It looked cold and refreshing, with something crimson bleeding through it.

"Non-alcoholic," he said, and nodded for her to try it.

She took a tentative sip. "Wow," she said, then took another. "What's in it?"

His blue eyes twinkled. "My special rescue recipe."

"Pomegranate?" Cassidy asked. She wanted to jump into her glass. It was that good.

He nodded. "And soda, with a little extra vitamins."

"*Gracias*," she said, savoring the cold, tangy taste.

The waitress from the table of surfers arrived with the bill, and Mel cashed them out.

"I went to Reeve's apartment," she said when he returned.

"Find anything?"

Cassidy shook her head. "It's been broken into. The whole place was trashed."

Mel grimaced.

"I met Reeve's neighbor," she said, wondering how to ask what she needed to ask. She looked at him, as if for reassurance.

Mel crossed his arms, the normal twinkle in his eye replaced by a worried, focused gaze.

"And he said that he and Reeve sometimes partied with 'the girls.' "

Mel frowned. "Did the neighbor know where he'd gone?"

Cassidy shook her head. She was starting to feel tired. "So how . . . ." She gazed into her drink. "These girls, these . . . *chicas*," she finished in a quiet voice. "How do people contact them? Where do they hang out?"

"Nowhere you'd want to be. That's for sure," Mel replied sternly.

Who had the man outside Reeve's apartment been waiting for? *Stop Selling Our Children.* Was he the girl's pimp? Her father? The thought made her feel sick. She gripped the edge of the bar and tried to breath deep and steady. *Please don't let me puke all over this bar.*

"Whoa, there," Mel said. Quick as a flash, he came around the bar. "Smell this," he said, lifting something to her nose.

Cassidy inhaled the strong scent of ginger, which cleared her mind instantly. After another slow breath, she felt better.

"Okay?" Mel asked, his hand steady on her back.

The gesture washed over her, bringing on a sense of loss so intense she had to clench her fists. This was what she missed—kindness, compassion, someone who was there to catch her fall.

What would it be like to have someone in her life who could care for her like that again?

She realized that Mel was still watching her with that concerned gaze, so she nodded.

Mel took a step back and leaned sideways against the bar.

"Reeve had a girlfriend—Jade," Cassidy said. "I think she was a prostitute." She glanced up at Mel. "Do you know how I could find her?" Even as she said it, the task seemed not only impossible but also dreadful.

"Listen," Mel said, scratching his chin. "Prostitution is legal here, but you don't want to go around looking for this girl. There's still a lot of crossover with illegal activity. It's an industry that makes a lot of money, and anytime you have that in a town like this, you'll find trouble."

Cassidy grimaced.

"Let me ask instead," Mel said, his eyes filling with kindness. "I might be able to find out something."

A pulse of relief washed through her. Cassidy pushed to stand but her legs wobbled.

A wave broke in the distance. Cassidy looked out across the bar, which was dark and empty, the candles extinguished.

Mel seemed to be watching her carefully. She thought of her empty room and its empty bed, her empty heart.

As if he could read her mind, he pushed off the bar and stepped close. His fingers brushed a hair off her forehead. *"Déjame,"* he said. *Let me.*

Maybe later she would regret this, but right now, she was in no place to resist the way he was focusing solely on her, like she mattered.

Cassidy stood and he took her hand. He led her slowly out of the bar and along the row of doors leading to her room.

The energy she felt seemed to increase with every step, so that by the time she was at her door, her fingers were shaking.

She fumbled with the key until Mel gently took it from her and slid it into the lock. He turned and took her face in his hands. Cassidy gazed into his blue eyes, unable to stop herself from leaning in to kiss him. He pressed his lips to hers in a soft, tender kiss.

Mel opened the door and led her inside. She stepped out of her flip-flops, feeling jittery. This was happening. There was something powerful about Mel's presence, something that drew her in. She unbuttoned his shirt as they kissed in the dark. His chest was warm and he felt so strong, as if he could scoop her up in his arms and carry her for miles. He kissed her softly, but urgently. She kissed him back, the sensation foreign and familiar all at once. As he kissed his way down her collarbone, she ran her hands through his hair, loose now, the silky feel of it stirring something deep inside her.

Everything fell away—her thoughts, her loneliness, her fears. Mel kissed her softly behind the ear and held her close—sparking a craving so powerful she felt dizzy. It felt so good to give in, to receive this kindness because hiding behind it was the pain of everything she had lost. All she had was this moment, so she focused on savoring each moment: his lips on hers, his breaths in time with hers, his attentive, gentle touch.

Afterward, they lay there together with her hand draped across his shoulder and her head on his chest. He made no motion to go, so she relaxed and listened to his breathing deepen, until her eyes felt heavy. She drifted off, still tucked into his embrace.

CASSIDY WOKE SLOWLY, the details of the day before returning to her in pieces. She was both relieved and apprehensive that Mel, breathing softly, was still there.

Her heart ached for the life she no longer had: Saturday mornings reading the paper alongside Pete, the silence broken only by slurps of coffee, but their bodies so close that she could feel his warmth. Was it something about Costa Rica that had made her so bold—*pura vida* and all that? Or had seeing other couples enjoying time alone in a beautiful place made her desperate to experience some of that joy too?

First, I danced with Héctor, she thought with a rush of tenderness. *Now I wake up next to Mel.* Recently, Cassidy's grief counselor had encouraged her to take more risks. *Well, I guess I'm a good listener.*

Light had filled in the cracks of the slatted blinds, and the frosted glass door was lit by a soft glow. Cassidy squinted at the clock, but the numbers danced in a red blur. She had slept with her contact lenses in and her irritated eyes refused to focus.

Mel rolled over and tucked his arm around her middle, exhaling a sound like a purr. "*Buenas días, preciosa,*" he said, kissing her temple.

Cassidy did not feel gorgeous, not in the least. She laughed and pulled his arm tighter around her.

"Let's stay in bed all day," Mel said, stroking her arm.

"What about the bar?" Cassidy asked.

"Screw the bar," he said. She peeked at his face but his eyes were still closed.

Cassidy rolled out of bed. "I need a shower."

"Can I help?" he asked, propping himself up on an elbow.

She knew it was silly to feel awkward after what they had shared the night before, but she did.

Mel's eyes turned gentle, as if he could read her apprehension. "You want me to go?"

"No," Cassidy said, a little too quickly. "Would you wait . . . a little longer?"

Mel gave her a nod.

By the time Cassidy returned from her shower, he had dressed in his khakis and linen shirt. They met at the door and he pulled her into a long embrace. He kissed her once, a gentle kiss that made her chest ache for more.

If Pete could look down on her from somewhere, would he be disappointed in her, or proud of her for trying to find happiness without him?

"I found this," Mel said, picking up a piece of paper from the top of dresser.

Cassidy vaguely remembered ignoring the scrap of paper on the floor the night before. It was a note from Bruce. Her gut quivered as she scanned it.

You're in. Meet at Bambu in
Playa del Coco at noon.

TEN

"THIS IS ABOUT REEVE, isn't it?" Mel asked.

She nodded. "Bruce is taking another boat trip to Nicaragua."

"You going?" Mel asked.

Did she imagine the look of concern in his eyes? "I kind of have to," she replied.

"San Juan is a little rough," he said.

Cassidy looked into his face again, wondering if she was stepping over some kind of invisible threshold by giving him permission to worry about her. "I'll be okay."

"Somehow I know you will be," he said with a smile. "Send me picture of you charging *más grande olas*, okay?"

"Okay," she said.

Mel gave her one last kiss, and then he stepped from her room and disappeared around the corner.

AFTER THE BUS dropped her in Playas del Coco, Cassidy hunted down the restaurant situated on the edge of the brown sand. She scanned for a table of rowdy surf rats but didn't see such a group.

Bruce had not yet arrived—she was a little early—so she ordered a cup of coffee and sat watching the young waitresses buzz around the tables.

Cassidy had woken early to use her last few hours of Wi-Fi to hammer away at her projects, then emailed her brother Quinn about her change of plans.

Ever since their father passed away when they were teens, they had established a pact to "be each other's person." Quinn ran a bar in San Francisco and was always training for some marathon or other, so he kept weird hours. They talked on the phone every few days, most often in the afternoons. Certainly never in the mornings when he was only just dipping into his good REM sleep.

She had cancelled her flight home and planned to wait to until after the return trip from Nicaragua to book a new one. The staff at Crazy Mike's graciously offered to store her extra gear and laptop while she was away.

Earlier, she had accepted Mel's friend request on WhatsApp, but he hadn't been at the bar when she walked through it on her way to catch her bus. It felt weird to leave without saying goodbye, but maybe that was for the best.

The bus ride had made her sleepy, but now that she was here, her mind was a spear ready to strike. But would she find answers on this trip, or more dead ends?

Halfway through her coffee, a petite woman slid up next to her at the bar. "You Cassidy?"

Cassidy gave her a wary nod.

The woman was deeply tanned, with dark wavy hair. She shot her a lopsided grin. "I thought so. Bruce told us to keep an eye out for you. He's running a bit late."

The woman extended her hand, and Cassidy shook it.

"I'm Benita," the petite woman said, and tilted her head toward a rectangular table situated in the shade, where a group of forty-something women were drinking cocktails and eating chips and salsa. "Come on, we ordered you a drink."

Cassidy picked up her bag and followed Benita to the table.

"Girls, this is Cassidy." She gave Cassidy a scrutinizing look. "Cassie? Cass?"

"Not Cassie. Cass is okay though," she said, relieved to have gotten that out of the way. She loathed Cassie—it sounded like a kid's action figure, or a line of cosmetics. She didn't tell them Pete's nicknames: CeeCee, Kincaid, or on special occasions, Kinney. Her gut lurched. Before his accident, she hadn't made up her mind about taking his last name.

The group gave her a rowdy greeting, and one woman passed her a glass containing orange juice with a blush of bright red floating like a cloud near the top. They toasted to epic waves and drank. The orange juice was fresh squeezed and ice cold and mixed perfectly with the tequila.

The group introduced themselves. Besides Benita, she met Marissa, Libby, Jillian, and Taylor.

"Glad to have you," Benita said, raising her glass.

Cassidy smiled. "Thanks for letting me crash your trip."

"Absolutely," Benita said. "Us surfer girls have to stick together."

"Have you guys done trips with Bruce before?" Cassidy asked, sipping her drink.

"Yep, two years ago he chartered us a boat in El Salvador."

"And he set us up with a killer spot at a new resort last spring—in Mexico. It was just us and these two hot local boys," Marissa said.

The group razzed her.

"You could have been their mama," Benita chided.

"Hey," Marissa said, grinning. "No harm in lookin', right?"

"Jared's not good enough for you?" one of them teased.

"Jared's her husband," Benita said to Cassidy. "He's a model."

Marissa, who could be a model herself with her long blonde hair and tall, slender build, rolled her sparkling blue eyes.

"Please, you guys are too much," she said.

"We usually do a trip a year, the six of us, except this year Michelle had to bail last minute. Her kid got appendicitis. Enter you

—her replacement. We all live within a few hours of each other, but life gets in the way, and we don't always get a chance to surf together."

"Where are you from?" Marissa asked, tying up her long blonde hair in a loose topknot.

"Eugene," Cassidy replied before thinking. "But I learned to surf in Ventura. I moved there when I was ten." She hadn't meant to say so much so soon. It must be the tequila.

Just then, Bruce arrived. "Ladies," he said with a little bow. "Everything's set. We're ready when you are."

In a flash, the women downed their drinks. Libby threw some bills down on the table, and the group collected their things.

Cassidy took a deep breath and followed them down to the water's edge. Was she embarking on the trip of a lifetime, or was this the final step towards some terrible truth?

THEY BOARDED THE *TRINITY*, Bruce's bigger boat, complete with three bunk rooms and a modest galley manned by a slight, dark-skinned older man named Jesus.

By the time they set out for a sunset surf session at wave up the coast, the afternoon sun pierced Cassidy with its harsh glare, but once they were underway, she went up to the deck to feel the breeze.

Half of the women were drinking beers, and all were busy donning sunscreen and zinc or taking photos. Cassidy jumped in to help get a group shot of them on the bow. The wind made small talk too awkward, so Cassidy settled in for the ride, watching the yellow cliffs pass in a blur.

Once they arrived at the surf spot tucked into a sapphire blue bay, Bruce idled outside the breakers, watching the sets carefully, while the women evaluated the surf. In the low light, waves exploded into piles of fluffy, white spray, each droplet turning into tiny shimmering pearls.

"Yeeeeew," someone belted out when a set broke.

"Let's do it!" someone else added, and just like that, the women were grabbing their boards and jumping over the side.

Cassidy was quick to follow, jumping in and paddling toward the lineup. She caught up with Benita, who grinned like a kid on Christmas morning.

"This is a world-class spot, man," she said. "Get ready for barrels."

THAT NIGHT, after a grilled fish dinner and several bottles of wine while anchored in the tranquil cove where they'd surfed earlier, the group dispersed, leaving her and Benita alone.

"I didn't get the chance to square up with you before we left," Cassidy said. "How much do I owe you guys?"

"Everything's already paid for," Benita replied with a wave of her hand. "You can pick up the tab in San Juan. We've only paid deposits on the rooms, and we'll probably run up a good bar tab. If that doesn't take care of it, we can work something out."

Cassidy would rather just pay the group and be done with it, but that would be impractical on the boat. Even back at the bar, what would she have done? She didn't travel around with a wad of U.S. bills.

"Okay," she replied.

Above them, tiny white stars spread across the black canvas of night, the mountain range on the horizon creating a sinuous black cutout. Waves lapping against the boat complimented the view.

"So do you work, or are you one of those trust funders?" Benita asked.

Cassidy laughed. "I work." She thought of her seismic stations up on the mountain. "I'm a volcano seismologist. I do research on Arenal."

Benita raised an eyebrow. "Should we be worried?" she said with a smirk.

Cassidy tried to play along, but this question always irritated her. "Not worried." She paused. "But prepared? Yes. Always."

"So is it gonna blow, or not?" Benita asked.

"No," Cassidy said. "At least, not today. Probably not tomorrow, either."

Benita laughed.

At the other end of the table, Jillian and Libby's conversation was getting heated.

"What do you do?" Cassidy asked, hoping to escape soon.

"I'm a lawyer," Benita replied. She nodded at the ring that Cassidy was unconsciously spinning around her finger. "You married?"

Cassidy almost choked on her own spit.

Before she could answer, Jillian's sharp voice cut in. "I'm not blind," she said to Libby. "I know it's her."

"How can you be sure?" Libby answered. "This is your marriage we're talking about here. Think it through."

"I *have* thought it through," Jillian replied, her voice trembling. "That asshole," she said, and broke down.

Benita slid over to Jillian and the three of them huddled together, Benita speaking in quiet tones while Libby held her. Jillian began to sob.

Cassidy carefully detached her sticky thighs from the bench seat and slipped through the side door, glad to drift away. Whatever drama going on was none of her business. Besides, it gave her an escape from talking about Pete.

She didn't want to go to bed yet. The rooms were deep below decks, and even with the air conditioning, the cramped space didn't exactly exude relaxation. Bruce was in the wheelhouse, which also served as his bedroom with a tidy bed built into the corner.

He popped his head out of the doorway. "Settling in?"

"This is a pretty nice boat," she said.

"Thank you," he said with a small bow. He rubbed his hand over the top of the dashboard, as if stroking a beloved pet.

"When will we get to San Juan?"

"Tomorrow we cross into Nicaragua," he replied, ticking off the days on his fingers. "We'll surf Pirate's, then Rosie's...so Tuesday evening."

Cassidy nodded. "Can I see Reeve's cabin?" she asked, suddenly curious.

Bruce rose. "Sure," he said, and led her down the steep ladder to the galley. The bunkrooms were located in the stern, past the kitchen and the tiny head. Jesus was drying dishes, his forehead beaded with sweat.

Bruce asked Jesus in soft Spanish if he could enter his room.

Jesus looked a little puzzled but nodded, extending his hand as if to say, "be my guest."

They opened a narrow door under the stairs that revealed a closet-sized room with a sloping roof. A bunk was built into the wall, with what looked like storage space beneath. A tiny overhead light shone above the narrow bunk, which was made up with crisp blue sheets, the top folded over and the pillow fluffed. Hanging across the ceiling was a mesh hammock containing a worn backpack and a small guitar-shaped case.

Cassidy stepped inside. Reeve had been here, slept here, then one day never returned.

"Did he take his things with him?" she asked suddenly, eyeing the hammock.

"He hadn't brought much, but yeah, it was gone."

"You checked?" Her eyes went to the cubby space beneath the bunk.

Bruce nodded.

"What about the video equipment, the camera?"

"That's all mine. He left it, thank goodness. That stuff's expensive."

She pictured Reeve hunched over a screen, editing images until late into the night. "Did he work in here?"

"Sometimes," Bruce replied, his face pensive. "It sort of

depended on what the day was like. He cooked, too, so he fit in the editing when he could."

Cassidy gave the room one more look, but couldn't sense Reeve's presence. The idea that she would was ridiculous, but it was still disappointing.

What had she hoped to find? A note with his itinerary?

Frustrated, she turned from the doorway. She had come on this trip with unrealistic hope of tracking down Reeve in Nicaragua, but a growing sense of doom spoke of the very real possibility that she would hit yet another dead end.

ELEVEN

AT EVERY LOCATION the group surfed over the next several days, Cassidy searched the shoreline for signs of life—a camp, roads, people. When they had company in the lineup, she asked about Reeve, but the surfers she met just shook their heads.

On their final morning before continuing to San Juan, she woke to the distant *shushhhh* of waves combing a beach and uncoiled from her sheets. After slipping on her glasses, she checked her watch—it was still early, not quite six o'clock. Not wanting to wake the others, she carefully slipped down the ladder, scooped up her duffel, and tiptoed to the bathroom. She pulled on her bikini top, board shorts, and a long-sleeved rash guard.

After putting in her contacts, she packed away the T-shirt and shorts serving as her pajamas, but spied the yellow hoody at the bottom of her duffel. She pulled it to her face, held it close to her cheek and closed her eyes. Although it didn't hold Pete's earthy scent anymore, it brought him back.

I miss you so much.

Just for a moment, she allowed her heart to swell with the memory of his tenderness. Her body ached to feel his strong arms around her, to feel his kiss on her lips. Her ring flashed in the dim glow of the bathroom lights, and she caressed its surface and gave it a slow spin around her finger.

Pete had designed it himself, right down to the peridot, a volcanic gem that no one else would choose for an engagement ring. A dull ache thudded low in her belly. *Whoever said time heals all wounds is a damn liar.*

She swiped her wet cheeks and stuffed the sweatshirt back into the bottom of her duffel, then hurried up to the deck.

A band of silky pink marked the eastern horizon, the sun's rays still hidden behind the distant mountain's silhouette. Bruce and Jesus were nowhere in sight. She squinted into the shadows towards the rocky beach. It was not yet light enough to see the wave, but she could hear its thunder.

Quietly, she unsnapped her board, then carried it to the ladder and slipped into the water. The ocean felt fresh and clean on her sunbaked skin.

The tops of the scraggly trees on shore were turning from muted gray to green as she paddled, with the sunrise warming to a soft orange.

When she neared the takeoff, she saw Bruce, his head just visible above the surface.

"You're up early," he said, smiling, his white teeth practically glowing in the low light.

Cassidy shrugged. "I'm not very good at sleep."

Bruce shook his head, snapping his wet hair from his eyes. It was the same gesture Quinn did when they surfed, and it made her miss her brother, with his cackly laugh, his pranks, and the way he always knew what to say.

"Sleep's overrated anyway," Bruce replied. "Especially on mornings like this."

The sun spilled over the land and basked them in its golden light. A cool breeze grazed the backs of the waves, peeling the tops back in a stream of mist that peppered her cheeks.

"So, how did you end up working on a volcano in Costa Rica?" he asked, squinting at her. "I mean, Hawaii has volcanoes, and aren't the Cascades volcanoes?"

"I spent a semester in Costa Rica during my junior year of college," she replied. "Back then, Arenal was erupting. I was already on a science track, but experiencing a real time eruption made me fall in love with volcanoes. I didn't think I would study Arenal, though. I would have been happy with any of the Central American projects, but it just worked out that way."

"So will you live in Costa Rica?"

"I couldn't live here," she replied.

"Why not?" he replied, eyebrows raised.

Cassidy searched for the right words. "Everything is 'Pura Vida' all the time here."

"What's wrong with that?"

She watched him for a moment to make sure he wasn't making fun of her, then shrugged. "There's no ambition. No urgency to contribute to the world."

"I have to predict earthquakes to contribute?" he teased.

"I don't predict earthquakes," she said quickly. "Nobody can."

"You know what I mean," Bruce replied, giving her a splash.

She realized she was being unfair. Of course, Bruce contributed —everyone needed an escape, a way to unwind and recharge. That had been her goal before that phone call from Rebecca.

"Just make sure you don't get so busy saving the world that you forget to enjoy it," Bruce said with a wink.

Pete had called her a workaholic more than once, but she had thrown the term right back at him. They would both often work late into the night, forgetting about making dinner until they were half-blind from hunger. Sometimes dinner would be a bowl of popcorn and a smoothie, or scrambled eggs with lukewarm beer. When Pete was writing, it was like he stepped into another world. It was the same for Cassidy.

"I'm here, right?" she said with more force than she intended. A set approached and Cassidy paddled forward, digging in with hard strokes. The wave lifted her up, and she punched to her feet, soaring down the face. She arced her body in a smooth upward turn, towards the center of the wall. Out of the corner of her eye, she saw her shadow appear, trailing her. Speeding water tickled her toes, and that playful optimism she so loved about surfing sprouted inside her.

The curtain over her head pulled back, basking her in beaming sunlight. Unexpected tears sprung from her eyes as she carved up and over the wave and flew over the back. *If only we could have had more time.*

BY THE TIME the lineup was filled with guests from the Trinity, Cassidy's head was beginning to pound from the lack of sleep and the glare of the sun, so she returned to the boat. After rinsing with fresh water and toweling off under the warm sun, she descended into the lounge. The rich scent of coffee filled her senses. She poured herself a cup, then hurried to her bunkroom where she downed some Tylenol and changed into shorts and a t-shirt.

While sipping her coffee, she dug out the papers she needed to proof. When she returned to the States, the pressure to publish would be immense—that and the reality of nailing down a job—a *real* job at a university. Had Héctor downloaded the latest data set yet? Would their seismic stations stay operational long enough for her to publish her findings next year? Sometimes looters would find her station, steal the car battery, solar panels, wires.

On her way back through the galley with her papers, Jesus looked up from where he was chopping peppers and onions.

"You play ukulele?" he asked.

Cassidy reached for a croissant piled among other pastries on a plate. "No, why?"

Jesus nodded toward his room.

Cassidy paused. "Hold on. You mean, you don't?"

"No," he said, shaking his head. He flashed his palm toward his doorway like an invitation.

Cassidy set her things down on the counter and stepped through Jesus's door. The bed was made as before, everything shipshape. Above her hung the ukulele case.

"Do you know Reeve?" she asked Jesus as goosebumps traveled down her arms.

Jesus smiled his big, soft smile. Did he nod? She couldn't be sure.

She placed one foot on the corner of his bed and braced her other leg against the wall, then reached up to the hammock.

"Just the ukulele?" she asked him as her fingers grazed the edge of the backpack.

"Sí," he said in his deep voice. "Mi bolsa," he said, meaning the backpack belonged to him.

After removing the ukulele from the netting, Cassidy hopped down to the floor. She perched on the edge of Jesus's bed and ran her fingers over the black, worn case. The clasps were weathered, maybe from the salt air; one was extremely tight and sliced her thumb when she pried it open.

Cassidy lifted the lid off the case to a polished ukulele resting inside black velvet. She put the case on the bed and removed the ukulele, then held it in her lap and strummed it once. The strings vibrated in a soothing hum, but it felt too loud for the small cabin. A peek inside the instrument revealed only a hollow cavity, but she shook it in case something was hiding deep inside. Nothing rattled or broke loose. Cassidy turned her attention to the case, but there was no hidden compartment, no false bottom. Disappointed, she put the instrument back in its velvet and closed the lid.

"Gracias," Cassidy told Jesus.

Jesus gave her a deep nod, then stepped to the side to let her pass. Cassidy carried the ukulele as a swarm of emotions filled her chest.

Reeve had taken his clothes and other personal effects, but not his ukulele. Were ukuleles expensive? Maybe Reeve didn't even really play it, but had just brought it along for fun. He had always dabbled in music. Maybe he was teaching himself how to play. If he had been going to San Juan to party, of course he would have left it behind. But if he had only gone into San Juan to get high or get laid, why take everything else and leave the instrument?

Unless Reeve had known he was leaving and wasn't coming back. Was that it?

She ticked off the possibilities. Maybe Reeve was running from someone or something in Costa Rica. If so, then why not just hop a bus and go over the border? Why abandon Bruce's trip and his responsibilities in San Juan? He would have known Bruce would fire him. Maybe Reeve knew he was taking a one-way trip to San Juan. If so, why bring the ukulele at all?

What if Reeve had left other things behind yet to be discovered? Though whether those supposed things would reveal why he left and where he was headed was unknown. Could she search the boat without making it a big deal? The other guests might think she was nuts. Bruce might not like her poking around.

"Cassidy," Bruce said from one of his wheelhouse windows.

Startled, she glanced at him. "What's wrong?" she asked, alarmed at his anxious expression.

"We've got company," Bruce said, nodding to the horizon. The he stepped out of sight.

TWELVE

UNNERVED, Cassidy watched a small powerboat painted with a blue-gray camo pattern emerge from the soft haze. Onboard, three stocky figures stood stoic in red vests and camo pants, one at the base of a large stationary gun at the bow. He stood with his feet planted wide, the brim of his hat pulled low over his dark eyes.

"Who is that?" she asked, but Bruce was on the radio, replying to whomever was coming towards them.

The boat slowed and maneuvered close to the *Trinity*.

"They're the Narc police," Bruce said, stepping forward to greet the men.

Cassidy hung back, but overheard the words for "documents" and "search" from the man in charge, his dark, square face a sea of wrinkles that tightened when he barked orders to his two subordinates.

They jumped aboard and began methodically opening storage spaces, calling to each other in short phrases, as if amped, ready for some kind of find. They passed by Cassidy with their charged, aggressive energy as if she wasn't there, and disappeared into the galley.

Cassidy's pulse thumped hard against her ears. These men had guns, and plenty of authority to use them.

Bruce handed over an accordion file of paperwork she had seen him use to store their passports. After settling on a chair at their dining table, the man removed their passports and studied each one carefully. Then he scribbled notes on a pad he pulled from one of his pants pockets.

The two officers down below were speaking to Jesus, then it was quiet again. Cassidy pictured the officers rifling through her backpack and the other women's belongings, touching their private things.

The man in charge stood and returned the passports and paperwork to Bruce, practically snapping his boot heels together. He said something sly, and indicated Cassidy with a jerk of his chin in her direction.

"*No, solo surfeando,*" Bruce replied, his jaw tight.

The two search officers returned. One gave his report—though too softly for Cassidy to hear it.

The lead officer turned to Bruce and asked, "*Donde están los otros?*"

Bruce indicated the beach with his chin. "*Surfeando.*"

The officer squinted in the direction of where the group was still out surfing and turned back to Bruce. He asked another question, to which Bruce's reply had a defensive edge.

The lead officer narrowed his eyes at Bruce, and then he was jumping back onboard his boat. The others followed. Seconds later, the engine started, the bumpers were pulled in, and they sped away.

Bruce remained standing, tracking the boat as it moved down the coastline. "Well, that was fun."

"Does that happen a lot?" she asked.

Bruce swept his hands to indicate the expanse of empty jungle and distant mountains. "Apparently inland from here, there's some kind of feud going on between clans."

"Are you worried about it?"

He gave her a sideways glance, his eyes stern. "I'd be stupid not to be."

Bruce kept his eyes focused on the retreating boat, now just a speck on the horizon. "Coke makes a lot more than tuna," he added.

Jesus poked his head up from the galley. Something wonderful was cooking; Cassidy could smell onions and melting cheese.

"*Se fueron*," Bruce told the old man.

Jesus nodded and disappeared back into the galley.

Cassidy swallowed hard. "What did they say about me?" she asked. "And why did you get mad?"

Bruce turned to look at her, his expression still tight. "It was nothing. He probably meant it to tease me, you know, here I am with six ladies all to myself." He sighed. "Typical machismo. These guys aren't exactly of the enlightened male outlook."

"At first I thought they might be pirates," Cassidy said.

"If they were, we'd both be dead," Bruce replied.

Cassidy sucked in a breath. She waited for him to downshift the tension with a joke or an offhand smile, but he didn't.

AFTER A SUNSET SURF session at another remote wave, Cassidy slipped to the bow of the *Trinity* with her stack of documents, hoping to pick up where she left off, but found fellow surfer Benita leaning back against the railing, playing Reeve's ukulele and singing softly.

Cassidy's gut lurched.

Benita stopped mid-strum, a look of concern on her face. "Is this yours? I found it on my bunk."

"Uh, no, I mean, yes, it's mine."

Benita gave her a shrewd look.

"You can play it. I don't mind, I was just surprised, is all."

"This is actually a really nice one. Do you play?"

"No," Cassidy said, settling in on her cushion. She realized that her answers were not making much sense.

"My son learned in school. He got really into it." She looked up. "Do you have kids?"

Cassidy tried not to sort through all the reasons why she did not. She hadn't even answered Benita's question the day before about her marital status.

"No," she said.

Benita shrugged. "It's the kind of thing that happens. Your kid gets into something, and then suddenly you're into it too."

"It's my stepbrother's," Cassidy said.

Benita fingered a few more keys and strummed. "The one you're looking for," she said. It was a statement, not a question. Cassidy remembered that Benita was a lawyer. A good one, too, she guessed.

Cassidy looked out at the blue horizon. The setting sun created a sheen of pearl luminescence on the water. From inside the boat, she caught the occasional whiff of baking bread.

"Yes," she said.

Benita gave her a look. "Are you guys close?"

"Not really," Cassidy replied, "but there isn't really anyone else who can look for him." She gazed at the distant charcoal-and-brown mountains shrouded in wispy clouds. "He was working for Bruce on one of these trips. He went ashore in San Juan and never came back."

Benita's eyes narrowed. "What did the police say?"

"I talked to the police in Tamarindo and Santa Cruz, but they said there wasn't much they could do because he disappeared in Nicaragua. I don't know if anyone's talked to the police in San Juan. My stepsister tried calling, but she doesn't speak Spanish. She has been talking to someone at the U.S. Embassy, but I don't think anyone's taking her seriously."

"Do you have an idea of what happened?"

"No," Cassidy replied, then the pieces of her so-called investigation played like a mind-movie behind her eyes. "Maybe."

"Do you want help?"

Cassidy looked at her sharply. Help? How could anyone help her with this?

Benita shrugged. "I handle sexual harassment cases, so I understand how to play dirty."

"Well, I don't know that there's any dirt, though...he's had problems with drugs in the past. Did some time in juvie." Cassidy remembered returning home from a college-scouting trip to discover that some of her things were missing, her mother's pearl-and-gold pendant among them.

Cassidy pulled her knees to her chest and gazed at the now-pink horizon. "He got in a fight with a taxi driver a few months ago. He was also apparently seeing a prostitute."

"You find her?"

"No," Cassidy replied as the sudden certainty that she was failing gripped her tight.

"No drug charges or activity?"

"I talked to his neighbor at his apartment." She shuddered. "And the surf guides he hung out with. No one I talked to reported seeing him doing drugs."

"Could he have been involved with the distribution chain somehow?" Benita asked.

Cassidy exhaled a slow breath. *Coke makes a lot more than tuna.* She knew from news stories that drugs moved from Colombia through Central America. Could Reeve have tried to smuggle drugs in order to sell them? Her skin prickled. Would he really be that stupid?

"Sorry. Let me know if this is too much," Benita said.

"No, it's okay," she said quickly. Before Pete died, his work as an investigative journalist led him to crack a few breaking stories. One thing he always stressed was that the most logical explanation was usually the right one.

"It's possible. Though that means he's probably . . . " The word faded before she could force it out. A tide of regret poured into her heart.

Benita strummed the ukulele a few times. "Could he just be traveling?"

"He promised my stepsister he'd check in. It's been almost three weeks."

Benita frowned. "What's your plan?"

"Visit the local police. See if they know anything."

"Then?"

Cassidy sighed. "Check the bars and the back streets."

"You packing?" Benita asked, her eyebrows arched.

"No," Cassidy huffed.

"We'll get Libby to go along. That girl can kick the crap out of just about anyone. She has this primal yell. Good God, it'll turn your blood to ice."

Cassidy fidgeted with her pencil. "You guys don't have to—"

"Forget it, okay?" Benita lowered the ukulele. "What did I tell you that first day? Us surf sisters have to stick together. And besides, what else are we going to do all day in San Juan? Sit around and drink margaritas? I mean, I'm looking forward to crashing out on a big, fluffy bed, but other than that, San Juan isn't exactly a dream destination."

Cassidy ran a hand through her tangled hair. Sitting on her duff drinking margaritas sounded pretty good, actually.

"And besides, you're picking up the tab, right?"

"Yes," Cassidy said. "Okay, if you really are sure . . . "

"Absolutely."

Cassidy tried to draw warmth from this unexpected offer, but Benita's company would likely make no difference to the outcome of this doomed errand.

THIRTEEN

IT RAINED DURING THE NIGHT, a hard, powerful cloudburst that tapped the roof of the cabins and bounced off the decks. In the lineup that morning, Cassidy searched for Reeve among the half-dozen surfers, but was not surprised when she didn't see him.

She asked the locals in Spanish if they knew of an American body surfer who may have passed through a few weeks ago. She had grown tired of the looks she had gotten when she first began her search—the fear and sadness. So instead of telling people she was looking for her disappeared brother, she explained that Reeve was an old friend she was trying to connect with. No one had seen him.

When Bruce anchored the *Trinity* in the calm bay facing San Juan del Sur, a quiver tingled through Cassidy's gut. What was she about to learn?

THE POLICE STATION was within walking distance from their hotel and she and Benita arrived after a short walk past brightly colored buildings and a mix of cramped businesses, apartments, and vacation homes.

The door to the baby-blue building stood open. Cassidy took a deep breath and entered.

A woman with a round face and hair dyed the color of straw greeted them in English. Cassidy had already formulated her question and asked if anyone could talk to her about a missing person's investigation.

The woman pursed her red lips, the top two points coming together in a way that reminded Cassidy of the evil substitute teacher, Miss Switch, in the childhood story.

"Would you like to file a report?" she asked.

"Would that help?" Cassidy asked.

The woman looked at her again, her quick eyes sizing her up.

"He's been missing for more than two weeks," she added.

The woman pulled out a small pad of lined paper. She asked a series of questions, jotting down Cassidy's answers: his name, age, height, hair and eye color, where he lived, his occupation, the date he was last seen.

Cassidy wished Bruce had come. He was the last person to see Reeve before he disappeared.

"Any physical characteristics?"

Cassidy's gut churned. *So we can identify a body?* she thought. "Not that I know of."

"Wait here," the woman replied, and disappeared behind the window. There were two rows of spindly chairs. She and Benita chose a pair against the wall and then sat.

"This feels like a waste of time," Cassidy groaned.

"Maybe, maybe not," Benita said with a shrug. Outside in the garden, an iguana stepped into the open and snatched a hibiscus flower from a low-hanging shrub. He devoured it in two flicks of his tongue and darted off.

Cassidy sat back and looked at the slow-turning ceiling fan and the layers of scrum visible on the mount. In the corner, a pair of geckos in the far corner rested, no doubt waiting for evening when they would feast on bugs.

A man in a uniform with graying hair and thick eyebrows stepped into the room, holding the pad of paper.

"Please," he said, then frowned when Benita also rose. "Who is this?"

"I'm her lawyer," Benita said, standing. The look she gave him blared, DO NOT MESS WITH ME.

"I assure you there is no need for this," the man said, his kind expression slipping a notch.

"Then you won't mind if I tag along," Benita said, her small body unmoving.

The man paused but only for a moment, then he extended his hand in the direction of the hallway he had emerged from.

"Please," he said again, and Cassidy and Benita walked a short distance to an open doorway. Inside, the officer's desk and chair faced two visitors' chairs.

"I'm sorry for your trouble," the officer said after they were all seated.

Cassidy couldn't hide her impatience. "Do you have any information about Reeve? And what might have happened to him?"

The man adjusted his posture, leaning forward on his forearms. "We received a call from the embassy," he said, his grandfatherly eyes connecting with Cassidy. "From your sister, yes?"

"Stepsister," Cassidy corrected.

"And we have no trace."

Cassidy grimaced. "I think something happened to him. Something unexpected."

"Unexpected things are known to happen. You party, you meet a nice woman . . . " he trailed off and shrugged, as if this was an enviable outcome. Maybe he had even dreamed of it himself. Fall in love and disappear in a haze of passionate lovemaking that lasts for weeks.

"He left something valuable on the boat. But his other possessions are gone."

The man was watching her as if trying to read her mind.

"Reeve has a history of using drugs," Cassidy said, knowing that it was important to say this even though it made her feel as if she were betraying Reeve somehow. "And I hear that there's a turf war going on," she added, picturing the narc boat.

The man's eyes flashed. "We do not allow the gangs in our town. They are off in the jungle, killing each other."

"Okay," Cassidy said. "But this is a resort town. Surely there are drugs, and dealers, and . . . "

"San Juan is like many resort towns in Nicaragua," he said.

"So have you looked into this possibility? That he got into trouble with drugs?"

The man opened his hands. "We have looked into every possibility."

The woman from the front window stepped into the doorway. She asked him something in rapid Spanish. Cassidy didn't quite catch the meaning, but there was an urgency to her request. The man frowned before turning back to Cassidy and Benita.

"We have used all available channels to find your brother." He gave them both a soft smile. "I'm sorry." He showed them to the entryway, nodded a cordial goodbye, and left. A moment later, a motorcycle engine revved up then faded away as the man drove off.

Cassidy continued walking, ready to leave the building, but stopped when the receptionist called out from behind the window. The woman looked both ways, her hands hidden from view, her made-up eyes trying to tell Cassidy something.

"MY SON, he is good with electronics," she began. "When no one comes to claim these things, sometimes I can give to him. To sell." Her chin lifted with pride, or maybe it was defiance.

Cassidy leaned to Benita. "Does she want a donation, or something?" she asked under her breath.

The woman placed a box on the window ledge and opened the lid.

Cassidy stepped closer to peer inside, her pulse a *pitter-patter-*

whump in her ears. Inside the box was a collection of phones, a few wallets, keys. She watched the woman for more explanation, but she evaded Cassidy's eyes.

Cassidy looked into the box again.

"Does anything look like his?" Benita asked.

Cassidy picked up a worn leather wallet and opened it. The slots for credit cards were empty. From another slot, she pulled out a worn card advertising plumbing services in Palm Beach, Florida and a rewards card for Sam's Club.

Cassidy had no idea if Reeve carried a wallet. She checked another wallet, a faux leather one in the shape of a rectangle but it was impossible to know if it was Reeve's.

With no way to verify the keys, she ignored them and turned her attention to the phones. There were three: an old-fashioned Motorola and two smartphones: an iOS and an Android. She tried the home button on both, but, of course, they were dead.

Cassidy wondered if Rebecca would know anything about Reeve's phone. The woman looked nervously towards the door.

"Do you know when these were found?" Cassidy asked.

The woman pulled out a sheet of folded paper from an envelope taped to the lid and read. She pointed to the Motorola. "*Octubre veintiuno.*" Then, she pointed to the Android. "*Cinco de noviembre.*" Then, the iPhone. "*Siete de noviembre.*"

Cassidy did the math and ruled out the Motorola, both because of the date it was found and its design. Reeve would have a smart-phone—if he hadn't sold it for drugs.

She looked at the remaining two. The Android was in a scuffed, black case. The iPhone's case was a sunset design: overlapping bright orange, pink and creamy white clouds wrapped around a mountain.

"Where was this one found?" Cassidy asked the woman.

She consulted her list again, and squirmed. She looked again at the door. "There was a stabbing. It was found in the dumpster behind the Uno station."

Cassidy wanted to drop the phone like it was contagious. "Who was stabbed?"

The woman ignored this question. "This was not found on the victim."

Cassidy turned the phone over, then back. "The victim wasn't Reeve?"

The woman shook her head.

"I guess it could be his," Cassidy said. "But I don't know. If I could turn it on, maybe the home screen would tell me something." She turned to the woman. "Do you have a cord?"

The woman paused, gave the door another anxious glance, and took the box away. She returned with a dirty, white cord and plugged in the phone to an outlet out of view.

In the distance, a motorcycle engine approached. The woman's face tensed.

Cassidy looked at the screen, but it was still blank. "Is it working?"

"Sometimes it takes a minute when it's really dead," Benita said.

The motorcycle engine's whir grew louder.

Cassidy pushed the home button, and the screen flashed a low battery signal.

The motorcycle engine noise cut off outside the station. The woman's eyes flashed with terror. She tried to grab for the phone.

"Wait!" Cassidy hissed, and pushed the home button again.

This time the screen flashed an image: it was a beautiful young woman, standing close to a brown-haired man wearing a sideways grin.

Reeve.

FOURTEEN

"YOU ARE STILL HERE?" a voice from behind them called, sounding mildly amused.

Cassidy whirled around to see the gray-haired officer.

Benita dashed toward him. "We wanted to find out if we can post a reward," she said. "We can make a poster, and you can put them up around town."

"A reward?" the officer asked, his forehead wrinkling.

"Yes," Cassidy added, "for any information that will tell us what happened to Reeve."

The officer seemed frozen on his feet. He looked from the woman behind them, who stood with a tight look on her face, and back to Cassidy and Benita, his full lips pursing. Something flashed in the officer's eyes. Greed? Fear?

"Do you have the reward?" he asked.

"Yes," Benita said. "Ten thousand U.S."

Cassidy gasped but covered it with a fake cough. Ten grand?

The officer shook his head, as if pushing away whatever his eyes had betrayed about his feelings. "I'm afraid this will only cause problems. We will get hundreds of calls."

"Maybe we'll learn something," Cassidy said, growing to the idea. She heard Rebecca's *You have the money*.

"No, this makes only work. For us." He eyed the woman behind them.

"Isn't that your job, though?" Benita said, stepping forward. "To do anything possible to find him? He's an American citizen. You don't want your town becoming ground zero for an international incident, do you?" She stared him down, her aggressive body language making her appear much larger than she was.

The officer put up his hands. "I have told you we have done everything we can. If you insist on offering a reward, I suggest you use your social media channels. This way, you can manage the information, and the payment."

"Will you tell your staff about it? Why don't we go call them right now," Benita said, motioning for them to continue to the office.

The officer's smile had completely vanished by now. "My officers would have already reported any information. This will be an insult."

"Their rights to feel insulted have long since expired. They should feel ashamed! An American disappeared in their town, and nobody knows a thing about it?" she said, her voice rising.

The officer took a step back, his face paling by the minute.

Cassidy was still standing near the window. She felt a soft tap at her back, and froze.

"You want those TV crews that filmed *Survivor* here to come back, right? To keep sending their rich friends here to spend money?"

"Of course," the officer replied.

"Then you better find Reeve," Benita said.

The officer threw up his hands. "We are busy with many responses each day. We cannot possibly devote our time to finding just one man. We did everything the embassy asked of us. We have no proof that any foul play is involved. He may already be in another country."

As casually as she could, Cassidy reached behind her back. Something hard and compact landed in her palm—the phone. But where could she hide it beneath a bikini top, board shorts, and a T-shirt? Her board shorts had a tiny hip pocket that would hold a few folded colones and lip balm, but not a phone. Slowly, she tucked it into the waistband at her low back, covered it with the hem of her T-shirt, and slowly lowered her arm to her side.

"C'mon, Benita," Cassidy said, interrupting the back-and-forth sparring between her and the officer. "I think we've done all we can here."

Benita turned and gave Cassidy a look, and it was so loaded—victory, aggression, power—that Cassidy actually felt it connect with something inside herself. Thank God for Benita. She tried to hold on to this gratitude, to feed off its strength.

"Talk to your officers. Tell them about the reward. Our group leaves tomorrow."

The officer's gaze flicked from Benita, to Cassidy, and back, as if he was wasn't sure if he should be relieved or disappointed that his sparring partner was leaving.

Cassidy headed for the door, trying her best not to show the officer her back. When she and Benita were outside, she breathed a shaky sigh of relief.

"My haircut wasn't until next week," the officer barked at the woman in Spanish.

"*Lo siento*," she said.

Cassidy and Benita moved down the street at a brisk pace.

"That woman gave you the phone, didn't she?" Benita asked under her breath.

"Yep," Cassidy said, tapping the back waistband of her shorts.

"Any idea how to unlock it?" she asked.

"No," Cassidy moaned. She hadn't thought that far ahead.

"Don't worry, I know a few ways."

Cassidy gave her friend a wary glance. "You're scary, you know that?"

Benita laughed. "Come on, let's get to work."

"UGH," Cassidy moaned from her perch at the poolside bar where she and Benita were huddled over Reeve's phone. "This is impossible!"

They had tried every combination of numbers to break into Reeve's phone: his birthday, his high school graduation date, and easy ones like "1-2-3-4" and "5-5-5-5" and the numerical code for his name. After more than an hour of attempts, Cassidy was beginning to lose hope.

Benita took another sip of her mojito. "Does Reeve have any hobbies?"

"Besides surfing, girls, and getting high?" Cassidy asked.

Benita waited.

"Sorry," Cassidy said. "Okay," she continued, more to herself than to Benita. She stared the phone, waiting for her minute of lockout to end while trying to think of new combinations to try.

"What are the things that are really important to him?" Benita asked, looking pensive. "Did he have any pets growing up?"

"No," Cassidy said. "His mom is allergic."

Benita seemed to think about this. "How about later, when he was on his own?"

Cassidy shook her head. "Not that I know of." Reeve could barely take care of himself, let alone a pet. "He used to be a big college basketball fan," Cassidy said, feeling like she was grasping at straws.

"Okay, which team?"

"University of Washington."

"Hmm, let's see if we can find some numbers." She picked up her phone and started typing.

"Favorite player?" Benita asked.

Cassidy thought about this but came up empty. Reeve had attended University of Washington for a few years. Maybe there was a player he liked while he was a student?

She typed a message to Rebecca, and her reply came almost immediately: Isaiah Thomas.

Cassidy showed her phone to Benita, who went back to work researching. Her eyes scanned several pages of text.

"Try 0-2-2-8," Benita finally said.

"What's that?" Cassidy replied while typing.

"His jersey number, which was two, and his all-time high score."

Cassidy entered but the phone remained locked. "Nope."

"Okay. Try 2-7-8-9. That's his birthday."

Cassidy typed the numbers then whooped. "You're a freaking genius!" she said to Benita as the screen unlocked.

The wave of victory ebbed as she realized what she was about to do. This was Reeve's life she was barging into. His privacy stolen.

"What should I look for?" she asked Benita with a sigh.

"Go to his photos," she replied, leaning over Cassidy's shoulder.

Cassidy opened the photo app. The last picture taken showed the same pose as his lock screen. He stood on a beach with his arm around a beautiful woman. Her thick, wavy hair fell past her shoulders, her shining, almond-shaped eyes set off by long lashes. Her smile stretched her young lips into a soft curve.

"Who's that?" Benita asked, sucking on a piece of ice.

"No idea."

Benita gave her a look. "His girlfriend?"

Cassidy stared at the photo, which had been taken in the pale light of dawn. Reeve looked...not happy, exactly, but calm, his smile bigger than his signature sideways grin. The beach they were standing on seemed familiar.

"This is in San Juan," she said slowly. "Look at the statue in the background."

"You're right," Benita said, pointing to the tiny white pillar just visible in the background, high on a hillside. "I remember seeing that when we came into the bay. Is there a date?"

Cassidy's heart did a flip as she read the top: November 4, 6:32 a.m.

"Oh jeez. It fits."

"Check his messages," Benita said.

Cassidy opened his WhatsApp. His chat history was full of messages from people with names like Wilfredo, Leo, and Carlos. She read a note he had sent to Rebecca on October 22nd, but it was short and to the point: Everything's beaut, sis! Pura Vida! He had placed a phone call that lasted five seconds to a number on the same date that he disappeared: November 4.

"It's going to take me some time to go through this. See if I can figure out if it means anything."

"If what means anything?" Bruce said.

Cassidy jumped. "Holy moly, where did you come from?"

Bruce grinned. "Did you think I'd miss the chance to enjoy a little R and R with you lovely people?"

The bartender appeared, and Bruce ordered a beer.

"Don't worry, I'm not going to crash your party," he said. "I'm just dropping off your flash drives with all the photos." He pulled out the tiny devices and handed Cassidy and Benita theirs. "I also wanted to remind you of your sunset tour of Mirador del Cristo, including the turtle release at La Flor."

"What turtle release?" Benita asked.

"There's a sea turtle refuge just south of town. Taylor set it up."

"Of course she did." Benita rolled her eyes. "They better serve cocktails."

Bruce nodded at the phone in Cassidy's hands. "You having trouble?"

"No," Cassidy replied with a grimace. "This is Reeve's phone."

Bruce's eyebrows arched. "How did you get your hands on that?"

Cassidy and Benita exchanged a look. Cassidy explained the series of events that led them to walk out of the station with the phone. "I think she felt guilty about keeping it when it could help us."

"Lucky for you," Bruce said. His beer arrived and he took a long sip. "Anything interesting?" he added, giving the phone a glance.

"Not really. He sent some texts the morning he disappeared. One phone call. And this," Cassidy showed him the home screen photo.

"Who's that?" Bruce asked, taking a long pull from his beer.

"Not sure," Cassidy said.

"His girlfriend?" Benita asked.

Cassidy studied the picture again. "How would she end up here if she lives in Tamarindo?" She turned to Bruce. "Do you recognize her?"

"No," Bruce said. "But I never met his girl, so..."

"It doesn't make sense. Why would Reeve hit the beach at sunrise and immediately hook up with a girl?" Cassidy said, shaking her head in confusion. "Tell me again the sequence of events. You guys came into port just like we did, after surfing. Did he go ashore with the group?"

"Yep, he drove the launch and dropped us off."

"He didn't come ashore?"

Bruce shook his head. "He had stuff to do on the boat." Bruce shrugged. "Nothing odd about that. It was his job."

"Did you see him on land at all during your trip? Did he stay at a hotel?"

Bruce laughed. "He stayed on the boat. Hotels aren't cheap, and I certainly didn't pay for a room for him."

Cassidy frowned at the photo of Reeve embracing the girl. "So he came ashore the next morning, but not to pick you guys up," she reasoned. "For some other purpose...like to meet this girl?"

"Could she have been a *chica*?" Benita asked. "Everything's done online these days. There are websites. He could have gone to one, picked her, and then met her at a designated time and place."

Cassidy shuddered. "Maybe?" She remembered the shaggy-looking man from across the hall at Reeve's apartment building. *Sometimes we party with the girls.* She tried to imagine Reeve clicking an image on a website, then taking that person to a hotel room. "But why at dawn and not the night before? Why take a picture of her?"

"She's a looker. Maybe he wanted to share it with all his buddies. That's a thing, by the way. It's like a trophy. He could have posted it on Snapchat or Instagram." Benita paused. "Though usually the girl is wearing less clothing."

"Ugh." Cassidy's stomach churned at the thought of something so demeaning. Was Reeve that kind of person? He had always been so passionate about things like fairness and freedom and even entertained conspiracy theories about the U.S. government meddling in places where they shouldn't. He was the kind of person who believed the myth about the first moon landing being a hoax. That was where Cassidy would step in with evidence to the contrary, and their debates would get heated.

Why would Reeve hire a prostitute and then want to boast about it? And what about the girlfriend back in Tamarindo he was so crazy about?

"Why is she smiling?" Cassidy asked, staring at the woman's face.

"She's about to get paid," Benita said in a low voice, then pointed to the WhatsApp call history. "What's this number, the pimp?"

Cassidy forced herself to think like an investigator. "Maybe."

"Did he call it before or after the photo was taken?"

Cassidy checked the record. "Two minutes after."

Benita sat in thought for a moment. "Huh. It doesn't really match up." She shook her head. "Try calling it."

"The number?"

Benita shrugged. "Why not?"

"With my phone or his?"

"Try his."

Cassidy looked to Bruce for input. "Definitely his," he said, his expression tensing.

"What?" Cassidy asked.

"Just . . . " He sighed. "Be careful, okay? Nicaragua can be a sort of . . . a free economy, if you know what I mean." He took in Cassidy's look of confusion. "Calling that number might set off a shit storm. And forget about the police being helpful in this. They're part of that free economy too."

"I wondered about that," Benita said. "The officer sure had a nice watch. And the woman's purse looked like an Adolfo Dominguez. I figured it was a knock-off, but maybe not."

"Okay," Cassidy said, her gut flipping over. "So should I call?"

Benita shrugged. "It's his phone, so it's not like whoever answers will know it's you."

"Right." Cassidy took a deep breath, then tapped the call button.

FIFTEEN

CASSIDY PUT the phone to her ear. The number rang and rang.

"No answer?" Benita said.

Cassidy ended the call and tapped her fingers on the bar.

"You said he had a history of drug use. Could it have been a dealer?" Benita asked.

Cassidy swallowed a lump of anguish. She knew Benita could be right. "That's a thing too, isn't it? Get high before you have sex." She closed her eyes. "I'm not cut out for this."

"Maybe take a break for a bit," Benita said, ordering Cassidy another drink. "Go for a dip in the pool. Get a massage. Put it out of your mind for a while. I'll take a look at it in the meantime. Go on." She unwrapped her pareo and draped it over the back of a lounge chair, then jumped into the pool.

"Do you know where the Uno gas station is?" Cassidy asked Bruce, ignoring Benita's advice.

Bruce thought for a moment. "Yep, just on the edge of the downtown."

"That's where they found the phone."

"You want to go there," Bruce said, after a long sip from his beer.

Cassidy put the phone face down on the bar. "Maybe someone knows something," she said, sipping from the fresh drink Benita had ordered her. "Around the same time that Reeve disappeared, a person was stabbed there."

"Not Reeve, though."

Cassidy shook her head.

"You're worried he was involved?"

Cassidy tried to picture a series of events that ended with Reeve at the scene of a stabbing. "I mean, back in Tamarindo he assaulted a taxi driver. What if something like that happened here? Only it didn't end in him paying a fine."

Bruce smoothed the bar top with his fingertips, then glanced at her. "Reeve didn't come across as violent."

"No weird behavior? He wasn't twitchy? Or spacey? Quick to fly off the handle?"

"No," Bruce said.

"You didn't notice anything missing?"

"No," Bruce said again, frowning. "He seemed like a good kid. A quick learner. Did everything I asked and then some."

Cassidy sighed. "I have to go down there." The sun was low on the horizon but they still had plenty of daylight remaining.

"I'll go with you," Bruce said, draining his beer.

A wave of gratitude washed over Cassidy. She knew the group would depart for their tour soon, and she would never dream of asking Benita to miss any more of her vacation. "Thank you."

"I can give you a lift whenever you're ready."

Cassidy took another sip of her drink for courage. "I'll just go change. Meet you out front in five minutes."

On the way to her room, she typed a message to Rebecca on her phone:

Heading to the place where police found R's phone.

Cassidy slid the phone into her pocket and entered the room. She hadn't bothered to unpack her things into the drawers. With such a meager wardrobe, why would she? She slipped off her bikini and reached for the mesh bag with her clothes, but paused because they were folded in the middle of the bed. She looked around for signs that the maid had been in the room, but the beds and carpet looked exactly the same as when they had checked in. *I must have taken out my clothes and just don't remember,* she thought.

Benita arrived, her wet hair slicked back and her pareo tucked tightly around her torso. "Hey," she said, sounding breathless. "Get this." She was holding Reeve's phone.

"I got into Reeve's banking app," she said.

"What? How?"

"It wasn't hard. He saved his password."

"Oh." Cassidy's stomach rolled into a tight knot. Was Benita breaking a law?

"Anyways, Reeve made a payment to something called Tikvah International."

"What's that?"

"I don't know yet. But he made it the day they left Costa Rica."

"Huh," Cassidy said, still not sure she understood where this was going. "How much?"

"Two thousand dollars," Benita replied, her eyes sparkling with excitement.

"Two thousand?" Cassidy echoed. She thought of his dingy flat. "How does a broke videographer find that kind of money?"

"Maybe he's not that broke." Benita shook her head. "I'll look into it more. Bruce told me you're going to where the phone was found?"

"Yeah."

Benita grimaced. "Well, here," she said, handing over Reeve's phone. "Maybe you want to show the picture to—someone who might know who the girl is."

"Right," Cassidy said, sliding the phone into her pocket.

She headed for the hotel lobby. Once at the front door, she had an inspiration and took out her phone.

She opened WhatsApp and tapped out a new message to Mel:

Reeve's phone was found in a dumpster where a stabbing had taken place.

He wrote back right away: And the police were generous enough to part with it?

She typed: Not sure generous is the right word. Do you know of something called Tikvah International?

Never heard of it, he replied.

Well, it was worth a shot.

What's your plan now?

Visit the site of the stabbing

Please tell me you're not going alone

I'm not

OK. Be careful

Cassidy gripped the phone and shook off her creeping anxiety. *I don't want to do this, but I owe it to Reeve to see it through.*

CASSIDY FOUND Bruce waiting astride a moped.

"What the heck is this?" she asked, unable to hold back her amusement at seeing his tall frame folded up on such a small vehicle —painted canary yellow at that. She had expected a car.

"It's the most genius mode of transport ever made, is what this is," he replied, unfazed. "Hop on," he added, and turned the ignition key.

Cassidy managed to slide one leg over the seat behind Bruce. There was nowhere to put her hands except around his waist. When Bruce pulled out of the hotel parking entrance, she had no choice but to reach her arms around his firm middle and hang on tight.

They traveled down a narrow street to a park facing a peach-colored Catholic church, then turned north, passing taco shacks, minimarts, T-shirt shops, and blocks of apartments. Though the streets were hushed due to siesta, within the hour the restaurants and bars would be full to bursting with tourists on the prowl.

Bruce reached an intersection with a broad boulevard that headed in the direction of the beach from the outskirts of town.

Across from the intersection stood a row of low buildings: a Falafel restaurant, a produce stand, and a whitewashed building with the name "Chabad House" painted in blue lettering. It looked like a community center, or a soup kitchen, and out of place compared to its neighbors.

Bruce turned right, away from the beach, swerving to avoid another moped leaving the curb. Cassidy tightened her grip around his middle.

The Uno gas station came into view. Moments later, Bruce pulled into the cobbled parking area in front of the glassed-in minimart.

Her stomach tightened. Was this where Reeve met his end?

Cassidy slid off the moped, and Bruce rested it on its kickstand. Cassidy looked around, walking slowly towards the side of the building where she had spied the dumpster.

The area around it looked unremarkable. There were no broken beer bottles or discarded cigarettes that she could sample for DNA. *Like they'd do DNA testing here,* she scolded herself. The packed dirt ground revealed no bloodstains. Cassidy did not attempt to lift the garbage-stained lid of the dumpster, rationalizing that the police had already cleaned it out.

She stood still and closed her eyes, hoping to feel some kind of epiphany. Had Reeve stopped here? Had he gotten into a knife fight, been injured or killed? Cassidy imagined Reeve's killer dumping Reeve's phone into the dumpster before the police came. It was possible.

The most likely explanation is probably true, Pete used to say.

But why would Reeve get into a fight behind a gas station? The only reason was drugs. Reeve had either been selling or buying, and the deal went bad.

A buzzing sensation caught her attention. It was coming from her pocket. She checked her phone but the screen was blank.

Reeve's phone was ringing.

She pulled it from her pocket. The WhatsApp number she had

called before, the same one Reeve had called the morning he disap-peared, was calling her back.

Cassidy looked for Bruce, but he had gone inside. She tapped the flashing icon on the phone.

"*Si?*" she answered, holding the phone with a light touch, as if something dangerous might pop out of it.

"*Tienes una entrega?*" a woman's voice asked.

Do I have a delivery? Cassidy thought, panicking. "*Si*," she replied.

"*Una hora,*" the woman's voice replied.

Cassidy's pulse whooshed past her ears as she tried to process what to say. "Where?" she blurted, but the call had ended.

Bruce joined her. "What was that?"

Cassidy groaned in anguish. "The number! They called it back." She brushed back tears. "It's drugs. He was making a delivery."

Bruce's face twisted into a grimace. "You sure? What exactly did they say?"

Cassidy relayed the conversation.

"Shit," he said, his eyes tense. He gripped his hips and sighed at the sky.

Cassidy stabbed the heels of her hands into her eyes. What would she tell Pamela and Rebecca?

"One hour," he said. "Here?"

"Maybe."

"Look, I know you're committed. But can I make a recommenda-tion?" he said, rubbing the back of his neck. "Now would be a good time to quit."

Cassidy blinked at him, realizing what the pinched look on his face meant: he was scared.

"I mean, what do you think's gonna happen?" he asked. "That they're gonna just tell you, 'Oh, yeah, that guy? We had to take him out.'"

Cassidy's stomach lurched.

"Sorry," Bruce said, as if reading her thoughts. "Maybe he's alive.

But he met someone and delivered something. Probably something illegal. The kinds of people he likely dealt with don't play nice."

The smell of the diesel fumes from the gas station coupled with the sour reek from the garbage bin was making her head swim.

"Sounds like you know something about it," Cassidy said, crossing her arms. Sure, this was dangerous stuff, and the phone ringing was like a hand reaching up from the underworld, but she had seen Reeve's world before and had never feared for her own safety the way Bruce seemed to be.

Bruce's expression didn't change. "Maybe I do. And maybe I'll tell you about it someday. But for now, I strongly recommend we skedaddle."

She crossed her arms and kicked at a pebble, letting his words bounce around in her mind. "Did you ask inside?"

Bruce shook his head. "They don't remember seeing anyone who fits his description, but he likely didn't buy gas or go inside. And the gas station was closed when the stabbing occurred. At least that's what they told me."

Resignation hit her like a cold splash of water. Cassidy's shoulders slumped. "So it's over?"

Bruce gave her steady look.

Cassidy looked around, imagining Reeve in a scuffle, the flash of a knife. Thugs dragging his body to its final resting place, wherever that might be. A lonely patch of desert? A crocodile-infested river? The ocean? Turning away from the place where Reeve had likely engaged in a battle for his life—and lost, Cassidy let a shuddering sob escape from somewhere deep inside her. She clapped her hand over her mouth, but the tears came anyway.

Bruce stepped close and gathered her in his arms. It was a gentle, kind embrace, and he didn't say anything, or try to stop her tears. Cassidy closed her eyes and imagined Pete doing the same thing. A wave of emotions rose up inside her, and she reached her arms around him and let the wave slowly fill her up then ebb, leaving her drained. Finally, she stepped back and wiped her eyes.

"I hate to do this, but I think we should get out of here. That phone call you made..." Bruce said with a grimace. In the low light, his brown eyes looked troubled. "...anyways, can I take you back to the hotel?"

Unease prickled the hairs on the back of her neck. Cassidy flicked her gaze to the left, then right.

"Are we in danger?" she asked.

"Let's just go," Bruce said in a tense voice, and hurried to the moped.

SIXTEEN

AS BRUCE SPED them down the main street, jumbled thoughts flipped through Cassidy's mind: Reeve, age ten, riding a wave into the shore on a boogie board, his grin bright and joyful; Reeve arriving home from school with one of his sidekicks to smoke pot in his room and listen to Beastie Boys at high decibels. Reeve at Christmas dinner, looking pale and quiet, and the rest of the family agreeing they should forgo alcohol this year. Reeve with wild eyes, showing up at her and Pete's house in Eugene, demanding money.

Then Cassidy pictured him at the beach in San Juan with the girl, his look peaceful, his eyes clear.

What had happened to him? Had he been clean, like he swore to Rebecca? Or had he slipped back into the party life and was making ends meet by delivering drugs to and from Nicaragua?

Would Reeve put Bruce in jeopardy like that?

Cassidy knew that when Reeve was using, his morals melted away like a spring snow. Nothing mattered except the next high. He had hurt so many people while locked in this battle.

But if he was delivering drugs, where did they come from? Cassidy had followed Reeve's abuse cycle enough times to know how the system worked, and the facts were off. Had he bought drugs in Costa Rica to deliver to someone in San Juan? If so, was he killed before he could make the delivery, and that's why his apartment was trashed? How did the girl play into the story?

Reeve had arrived in San Juan, stayed aboard the *Trinity* that afternoon, and come ashore early the next day. He had snapped that picture with the girl, then made a call. Later that same day he didn't show up to drive the group back to the *Trinity*. That night he calls her. The next day his phone is found in a dumpster at the scene of a stabbing.

It all seems jumbled, she thought, hugging Bruce's middle tighter as they made a turn down a narrow lane. Cassidy wondered if she would ever know the truth.

They paralleled the beach, the sun approaching the watery horizon. Soft orange light washed over the bars and trinket carts lining the street.

An engine revved behind them. At the same instant, she saw Bruce's expression in the side mirror tense. She turned. A small tan car with tinted windows looked to be moving swiftly towards them. She expected Bruce to pull over to let them pass if they were in such a hurry, but he accelerated. Cold fear pooled in her belly.

"Damn it," Bruce cursed over the engine noise.

"What?" Cassidy replied. The car behind them came closer.

"Not good, Cassidy. That car has been tailing us for a while."

A jolt of panic raced through her as the tan car began to overtake them. The car's engine whirred in her ears as the front right corner inched closer to her left leg. The car was going to force them off the road!

"Hang on!" Bruce yelled.

Cassidy squeezed him tight as he slowed suddenly and turned into an alley lined with dumpsters and boxes and black garbage bags cinched tight. Cassidy yelped as the back tire skidded, but Bruce regained control, and they sped straight, faster than Cassidy knew was safe. She turned to see the tan car speeding towards them, barely fitting through the narrow space.

"Who are they?" she yelled.

Bruce shot out of the alley and turned left onto the busy street lining the beach. Brakes squealed and horns honked as they cut across traffic. All around them people were walking, sitting in bars, riding in taxis. Music played from the restaurants and mixed with the sound of outboard motors buzzing in the bay.

Behind them came the sound of screeching tires and crunching metal. She turned to see a motorcycle on its side and a car stopped on the sidewalk. Honking and yells erupted from passersby as the tan car careened through it and raced after them.

"Shouldn't we call the police?" Cassidy cried.

"Those guys might *be* the police," Bruce yelled back.

Bruce took a sudden left into another alley, then a right onto a side street. Adrenaline poured into her bloodstream; she held Bruce's middle tight. He turned again, this time onto a narrow walkway meant for pedestrians headed for the beach. People jumped out of the way and yelled at them. Cassidy looked back, but saw no sign of the car. Could the police really be chasing them?

The path emptied onto a crosswalk that traversed the main street to the strand. Bruce drove across it, weaving between the people who jumped out of the way, their eyes wide with fear. A group of guys shouted curses as they darted between two restaurants to the sandy beach.

Bruce pulled up along the backside, hidden from the street. The low sun cast a warm, soft glow over the sand, turning it golden and sparkly.

"Can you get to the boat?" he asked.

"Like, swim?" she asked.

"Maybe you can catch a ride on that," he said, nodding at a large catamaran rocking gently in the shallows. A sandwich board placed in the sand advertised whale watching tours, and a line of people were waiting to climb aboard.

"Okay," she said, dismounting.

"Give me his phone," he said.

"Why?"

"Because that's how they found you," he said.

She slipped Reeve's phone from her pocket and handed it over. He popped open the back and slid out the battery. "Want me to take yours too?" he asked.

Cassidy shook her head. "My case is waterproof." She looked behind them but there was no sign of the tan car. "What are you going to do?"

"Follow that car." He must have seen the look in her eyes because he added, "I'll be fine. I'll meet you out there later."

Her fear deepened. Goodbyes were never good, and this one felt terrifying. What if Bruce got hurt?

Above them on the street, she heard the *swish* of a fast car. Bruce's jaw clenched. "That's my cue," he said, and sped off after the car.

Cassidy stood in the shadow of the restaurant, trying to control her breathing. She was shaking, with goose bumps pricking her arms and the back of her neck. Who had been following them? Had the phone call to Reeve's phone set it off? And what did they want? Was she putting Bruce in danger?

Cassidy hurried to the water's edge, lining up with the other tourists for the whale watching tour. Would they get her close enough to the *Trinity*? Could she jump off without being noticed? She stepped aboard, realizing that she would have to swim to the *Trinity* in her clothes.

The catamaran pushed off from the shore and the sails filled. The others on board ooh-ed at the sensation of gliding across the water.

Cassidy found a place on the back pontoon and sat, watching the shore lights fade, her thoughts swirling.

If Reeve was dead, why was she being chased?

Music from the catamaran's speakers drifted across the decks. Beer tops cracked open and conversations swirled. An announcement sounded with details of the tour: what was included, what kinds of whales they might see.

Cassidy's thoughts returned to the phone call. *Una hora*, the woman had said. But where? Cassidy checked her watch. She had another twenty minutes until whoever had called would be expecting Reeve to meet them.

Cassidy thought about this. Reeve had paid Tikvah International two thousand dollars, for drugs or something else illegal. And then he picked it up in San Juan. Then something went wrong. Had Reeve double-crossed his source? If so, why would they call him back? They would know that he was a crook. And they would know that he was missing because they would have been the ones to make it happen.

Or had they been?

Several facts came together at once, so fast the shore lights swirled, and before she knew it, she was sliding into the ocean and swimming back to shore.

As a teenager, she had completed the grueling junior lifeguards program. It was the only way her dad and Pamela would allow her to go to the beach and surf without supervision. Junior lifeguards had taught her about rip tides and currents, and how to navigate, how to know when you needed a rest, and how to signal for help. She also learned endurance. Most people drowned because they gave up, not knowing that they had the inner reserves to save themselves. As long as the water wasn't cold, it was possible to stay alive in the ocean for hours, sometimes even several days.

The water in the bay was inky black, with the lights from the town sparkling over its calm surface, and her pale limbs swishing beneath her looked ghostly. She removed her flip-flops and slid them onto her hands, both to keep them from floating away and to assist in her mobility. She started with breaststroke to get clear of the boat, praying that nobody noticed her absence while listening for worried voices calling to her, or for some kind of alarm. Then, sure she hadn't been noticed, Cassidy switched to freestyle, pausing now and then to check her progress, careful not to open her eyes underwater so as not to lose her contact lenses. Cassidy was beginning to wonder if indeed she was caught in some kind of rip current when the details of the restaurants and people strolling the beach began to sharpen.

Finally, dripping wet, she emerged from the water. Huffing, she bent over her knees and glanced around her, sure someone would be watching and sound the alarm. But she was safe in the darkness.

She squeezed out her hair and wiped her face, still watching for the shadows to jump out at her. With a quick pause to slide her feet into her soaked sandals, she set off towards the streets.

SEVENTEEN

CASSIDY WRUNG OUT the hem of her t-shirt and watched the busy thoroughfare for signs of the tan car or anyone who might be watching her. She imagined a stocky man in a dark suit picking his teeth with a switchblade, his steely eyes glued to the water's edge.

A steady stream of people strolled the streets: a mix of tourists in bright vacation wear and flip-flops, sunburned and in various stages of inebriation; and locals, the women in tight jeans and tops, wearing worn flats or heels, and the men in soccer-style sweatpants or faded chinos and T-shirts. The locals seemed to be in no hurry, stopping to chat, while the tourists rushed here and there, as if their vacation was a checklist with an endless column of boxes.

Linking shadows, she moved toward the Uno station, slipping between groups of tourists strolling or celebrating, their laughter and chatter mixing with the sounds of the traffic blazing by. Though her clothes and hair were soaked, no one gave her any special attention. At every corner she made sure to scan for a tail or anyone who looked suspicious. Could it be that no one was looking for her?

Where was Bruce? Had his plan to follow the tan car led to

answers? She trusted Bruce to take care of himself, but it didn't stop her worry.

Finally, Cassidy stepped onto the cracked sidewalk along the road leading out of town. She moved purposely, but kept her eyes alert. Maybe she was being paranoid, but her pounding heart told her otherwise.

The warm night quickly dried her sandals, so at least they stopped squeaking, and her hair no longer felt plastered to her head. She passed a *mercado*, its faded orange awning draped over the open counter offering bananas, papaya, and pineapple, then the white-washed synagogue with its faded star of David. The narrow artist's shop next to it was closed for the day.

Cassidy stopped at the corner across from the Uno, scanning the parking lot for some kind of activity that could be related to the call to Reeve's phone. According to her watch—her hour was up.

She shifted her feet on gritty sidewalk. The Uno might not be the meeting place, but with no other leads, she had no choice but to wait.

A tingle of nerves raced over her skin. What would she do if someone actually *did* show up?

Was she completely nuts for coming here? She remembered Benita's comment: *you packing?*

Across the street, several groups of young, backpacker types entered the Chabad House. Cassidy wondered if the synagogue doubled as a hostel, or some kind of community center. Could there be that many Jewish tourists in Nicaragua?

Across the street, the *mercado's* television blared some kind of telenovella. Cassidy could just make out the flashes of color, grainy from her vantage point.

She checked her watch again and grimaced. Ten minutes had passed since her meeting time. Still she waited, watching. Cars and trucks at the Uno came in; drivers filled their tanks, then drove off. The night air chilled her damp skin. Finally, after another fifteen minutes, Cassidy admitted defeat.

Coming back had been a long shot, but deep down she knew not doing so would have broken her.

She gazed around her one last time to make sure nobody was in the shadows, watching, then set off toward the center of town.

Bruce might already be back at the boat, waiting for her. She slipped her phone from her damp pocket and checked her screen. Nothing. Was he still following the tan car?

She veered around a foursome, each of them licking ice cream cones. When she passed them, ahead on the sidewalk stood three men talking in front of a car with the hood up. Two of the men were talking loudly, gesturing to the vehicle. One of them caught her looking and glared. The hairs on the back of her neck prickled.

Cassidy crossed the street, then fell in behind a large group of teens with a pair of adults that she assumed were chaperones. She stole a look over her shoulder at the men still arguing, but she couldn't see them now because of the propped up hood. Were they watching her?

Her breaths came faster inside her chest. What if they had been planted there to grab her when she passed? Or what if they were right now relaying a message to someone planning to intercept her later on?

The group of youngsters in front of her disappeared through the synagogue's open doorway, and Cassidy, thinking quickly, followed them.

Inside, a small entryway led to a large open room set up with long tables, where a banquette-style meal was taking place. Half the tables were full, a handful of the guests wore yarmulkes. A quiet hum filled the room from the conversation and clatter of silverware.

Servers wore white sleeveless tunics and black pants. A tall man with a frizzy white beard and dressed in a long, black ensemble moved about the tables, greeting and nodding to the diners. Even though Cassidy had never actually seen a Rabbi in person, this man had to be one.

A young man with dark hair, large glasses, and a wiry beard

greeted the group in front of her. "Welcome to Chabad House," he said. His accent sounded slightly off, neither English nor Spanish.

After a brief exchange, the group moved toward a set of open chairs.

Cassidy glanced behind her through the doorway to the street, but she couldn't see the men. Was she safe to keep walking? Or should she wait for them to leave?

"Please, join us?" the young man with the beard said to her.

Startled, Cassidy turned back. The young man swept his hand in a welcoming gesture toward the busy dining room.

"Um, no, thank you," she said, noticing an exit on the far side of the room to what must be the kitchen. Could she get through there to a back alley?

"Could I possibly have a glass of water?" she asked, swallowing the dry, salty lump in her throat.

The bearded man's eyes twinkled. "Of course," he said, and stepped away from his hosting podium.

Almost instantly, a young woman in a floral-print dress and black flats came from a side entrance with a glass of ice water. Behind her trailed a toddler, her curly black hair bouncing with her steps, her free hand dragging a ragged stuffed elephant.

"*Bienvenida*," the young woman said with a generous smile as she handed Cassidy the glass.

"Thank you," Cassidy said, and took a long sip.

The young woman scooped up the little girl, her chubby legs straddling the woman's hips and her head tucking under her chin.

Cassidy glanced at the truck with the hood up across the street, then back at the woman. "So what exactly is this place?" she asked, hoping to stall for a few more minutes.

The woman did not seem surprised at the question. "We are a Jewish emissary."

The woman must have seen the curious look on Cassidy's face because she continued.

"We have kosher meals, like the one we are hosting tonight." She paused to indicate the boisterous roomful of diners. "And classes and a synagogue. We also do important community service."

Cassidy took another gulp of her water while taking in the space.

"Would you like some latkes?" the woman asked, her eyes hopeful. The toddler began to suck her thumb. As if on cue, the woman immediately began to sway.

A poster on the hallway wall caught Cassidy's eye. It was another anti-human trafficking message. "Um, no thanks," Cassidy mumbled, stepping closer to read the wording on the bottom.

A sudden, overpowering sense of vertigo hit her when the connection fired in her brain. The water glass smashed to the floor. Cassidy jumped back with a startled cry.

"Oh!" the woman said, setting the toddler down and stooping to pick up the glass. The toddler instantly began to whimper.

Cassidy joined her. "I'm so sorry," she said, plucking the shards from the puddle.

"It's all right," the woman said in a kind voice, shooting the toddler a warning look. Cassidy and the woman collected all of the glass, then the woman piled the shards into the base of the cylinder and stepped from the room to throw them away. When she returned, she was carrying another glass of ice water. Even though Cassidy wasn't thirsty anymore, she took it.

With shaking fingers, Cassidy touched the logo stamped in blue ink along the bottom of the poster.

Tikvah International.

She had assumed Reeve had been selling drugs for them, but... here? Among these kind people?

"Um, can you tell me...what is Tikvah International?" she asked the woman, who was swaying in softly with the child on her hip again.

The woman's smile shifted to what looked like a grimace, but only for an instant. "That has become our most important purpose here," she said, lifting her chin with what Cassidy immediately recognized as pride. "Tikvah International is a rescue organization.

We take in victims of human trafficking and transfer them to safety."

More connections fired in her brain, but none of them made sense with the information she had. "Victims from here?"

"From all over Central America."

"How does it work?" Cassidy asked, her pulse racing.

"We have a hotline," the woman answered, but her reply seemed lacking, like she was holding something back. "And we have a network of volunteers who respond."

Cassidy thought about this. "My stepbrother, Reeve, made a donation," she said finally.

The woman bowed her head. "We are humbled by his generosity."

Cassidy had used Reeve's name on purpose, hoping for some kind of recognition, but nothing noticeable had registered in the woman's eyes.

Cassidy gazed at the poster, which showed a young boy dressed in a grubby shirt, turning back from a doorway, his pained eyes crushing her with their desperation. She noted the phone number printed at the bottom. It didn't match the one she had called earlier, but that didn't necessarily mean there wasn't a connection.

Why would Reeve have donated money to this cause? He had been in San Juan to sell or buy drugs. Had he needed a way to offload some cash? Had he eaten here and been inspired to make a donation by this very poster? That wasn't unlike the impulsive Reeve she knew.

Or was there something deeper going on, and he really wanted to support Tikvah International's efforts?

"Does Tikvah mean something?" Cassidy asked.

"Hope," the woman replied. She looked so peaceful standing there with the child cuddled close to her body and her life's purpose laid bare that Cassidy had to look away.

"Thanks for the water," Cassidy said, putting down her glass on a nearby table.

"Come back anytime," the woman said.

Cassidy looked both ways before stepping outside, but the arguing men were gone, the streets dark. She hurried down the sidewalk, her mind turning the facts over and over.

Reeve had paid money to a Jewish rescue organization—why?

Could Reeve have been involved in human trafficking somehow, and supporting Tikvah International was an atonement? Cassidy shook her head. No. That was too far-fetched, even for Reeve.

She thought it through again from the beginning. Reeve made a donation from Costa Rica, and then he boarded Bruce's boat. After arriving in San Juan, he went ashore and met up with a mysterious girl. Then he made a phone call to someone whom he likely met in order to sell something. That evening, he called—of all people—Cassidy. And then he disappeared.

She felt *this close* to unraveling the truth about Reeve's disappearance. What was she missing?

EIGHTEEN

WHEN CASSIDY FINALLY ARRIVED AT the beach, she paused, looking both ways before continuing toward a cluster of fishing pangas. After haggling for a price with one of the boatmen, she handed over a roll of damp bills, and with a hard push-off from the sand, he started the motor and they sped away from the shore. Cassidy sat low in the bow, watching for anyone who might be in pursuit, but there was no one. Soon the hush of cars passing and the music from the bars faded, and it was just the sound of the panga's engine and the water rushing past the hull.

As the cluster of anchored boats appeared, Cassidy searched for the *Trinity*. They passed a giant sailboat, the decks empty of people, the masts with huge sails rolled up tight. Only the bare bulb high on the mast and several running lights were illuminated. Cassidy imagined what sailing such a ship must feel like—the wind pulling the huge boat along as if by magic. The next boat was two rafted together with a party underway on the bigger one. In their little panga, Cassidy and her driver passed by unnoticed.

Finally, the *Trinity* appeared. After a week of paddling up to it after surfing, she identified the shape of the bow and the wheelhouse's silhouette easily. Her chilled body shuddered with relief. Before climbing the ladder up to the deck, she looked around to make sure no one, neither an occupant of one of the neighboring boats nor some pursuer, happened to be watching. Seeing no one, she slipped quietly onto the deck.

Onboard, everything was silent. A shiver traveled down her spine. She stood still and waited for a sound, some indication that Bruce was here.

A shadow moved, and she spun away, but the shadow caught her. In a flash, she was pinned to the floor by a heavy weight. She thrashed and kicked and was about to scream, but Bruce's voice stopped her.

"Cassidy?" Bruce said, his face hovering inches from hers. He jumped off her just as fast as he'd tackled her, and helped her up. "You scared the crap outta me."

Rubbing her wrists where his grip had chafed her skin, she slumped onto the bench where she had eaten breakfast just a day before. "Who did you think I was, anyway?" she asked.

Bruce put his hands on his hips. "Sorry," he said with a grimace. "Where were you? I was worried sick . . . "

Cassidy scrubbed her face with her hands. "I went back."

"You what?"

"After you left me on the beach, I got on the boat like you said." She swallowed, gathering her courage. Would he understand? "But then I got off. I had to go back."

His expression darkened. "What the hell did you do that for?"

Cassidy sighed. "The deadline for the meeting was approaching, and I just thought...I don't know...that it was my last chance to find out what happened to him."

"And did you?"

"No," she said.

Bruce paced the deck. "That was reckless, Cassidy. You could have gotten yourself killed," he said.

Cassidy swallowed hard. *Killed?* Surely, he was just trying to scare her. "It's not like I went out there and waved a flag, making myself obvious. Nobody saw me."

He turned to face her. "These people don't play games, Cassidy."

"I get it, okay?" she said, her voice rising. "I was careful."

"No," he replied, shaking his head. "You were lucky."

The confrontation hung in the air between them. Finally, Cassidy said, "I'm going to change into dry clothes."

Most of her clothing was at the hotel room—but she did find a bikini she had left drying on her bunk and a pair of shorts. And Pete's hoody. She reached for it, as if for a lifeline, and buried her face in its softness. Her heart responded with a memory that made her breath catch. They'd gone surfing at a remote Washington beach, then built a bonfire after. Pete loved sleeping under the stars, and though it made her nervous to be so exposed, she had curled into him with the fire crackling and popping and the stars blinking from the dark night.

How many more memories like that would they have made?

A lifetime of them.

BRUCE WAS IN THE GALLEY, pulling items from the fridge: onions and peppers. Garlic from the hanging basket over the counter. A bag of fresh shrimp, which he placed in the sink. She was relieved to see his stern look gone.

"Hungry?" he asked.

Even though she hadn't once thought about food, Cassidy felt a nauseous tickle scratch at her insides. "I think so." She leaned her hip against the counter. "How can I help?"

He glanced at her. "Can you peel shrimp?"

Cassidy moved quietly to the small sink and began peeling, making a pile of the limp gray crustaceans in a bowl he placed next to them. The simple task made her feel purposeful, and she gave herself to it. The shrimp's tiny feet would sometimes peel away perfectly, but usually they broke off and she would have to go back and pluck them from the meat.

Her mind drifted back to her visit ashore, how she had waited in the shadows, scrutinizing the activity at the Uno station for anything out of the ordinary. No car came at the arranged time, no shady characters lurked on the corners.

Bruce added the peeled shrimp from her bowl to the hot frying pan. The meat sizzled and the scent of seasoned onions and garlic wafted past her nose.

"So, we'll stay here tonight. Head back tomorrow and coax the ladies from their big fluffy beds," he said, his voice light. "And drag Jesus from his family reunion."

Cassidy saw through his attempt at humor. He was just as preoccupied as she was.

Bruce served the food onto two plates, and she followed him to the deck where he placed them on the table. Her stomach responded with a shuddering rumble. He retrieved two beers from the outside fridge and cracked the lids.

Cassidy took a bite of the fajita and her taste buds nearly popped off her tongue. They chewed in silence for a while. She took another bite.

"When did you first discover that Reeve was an addict?" Bruce asked.

Cassidy drew a deep breath at the sudden recollection. "When he was thirteen. We were on vacation at a ski resort. The condo belonged to a friend of Pamela's, and Reeve broke into the locked liquor cabinet. He was drunk every night."

"Did your dad and stepmom know?" Bruce asked, taking a bite.

Cassidy shook her head. "I don't think so." Rebecca knew, though. She had known all along.

"Was it just booze?" Bruce asked.

"It started there, then it was pot for the longest time. All through high school. Then in college he started dealing. You know what's funny? He seemed to function okay for a while. I mean, he was no star student, and he was always a little unpredictable, but it was like those drugs became a part of his coping mechanism, and they worked."

"Plenty of people are casual users. Did something happen?"

Cassidy set down her fork. "Yeah. Meth. He dropped out, and everything sort of snowballed from there. The last time I saw him he threatened me. Pete wasn't there. I had to call the police."

"Who's Pete?" Bruce asked.

Cassidy's sluggish brain tried to scamper back in time. "Uh," she managed.

Bruce watched her with an odd expression.

Cassidy closed her eyes and bit back the flood of pain. Forced the words past her teeth.

"Pete was my fiancé," she managed. "He . . . passed away last year."

They're only words, Cassidy told herself. She had practiced saying them with her grief counselor in an effort to make them flow easier. It hadn't worked. She could count on one hand the number of times she had actually spoken these words aloud. Either someone else shared the information for her, or she avoided having to say it. Evasion was a special skill that she was perfecting to an art.

"Oh jeez," Bruce said, wincing. "I'm so sorry."

The water lapping the boat's sides and the muted music from the rafted boat party filled the silence between them.

"Do you mind telling me...how?" he asked, the wrinkles around his eyes crinkling with empathy. "I mean, you . . . he . . . you're so young."

She gathered a breath and held it, then with the exhale, the words tumbled out. "He was in an accident . . . "

Bruce grimaced. "I'm so sorry, Cassidy."

Cassidy had nothing to say. She put the California Highway Patrol's photos of Pete's accident scene out of her mind with images that her grief counselor had helped her create to push them away: Pete at the bottom of the ski lift, wearing his puffy blue ski coat and shiny blue ski boots, leaning forward against his poles that were planted in the snow. Pete, hard at work building her a set of raised beds for their lettuce and peas, the late-afternoon sunshine casting long shadows. Pete, sitting across the table from her in their home late at night, rapt with concentration as she shared her latest geologic breakthrough with him. It might be the thing she missed most: being able to share what was in her crowded brain and have him understand, engage, and discuss it with her, even challenge her, and then after, taking her to bed.

What most people never understood was how hard it was *not* to talk about Pete. It was especially awkward in the geology department. She was new enough that she had no deep friendships, and she feared that everyone regarded her as the "girl whose fiancé crashed his motorcycle." Every now and then some detail about Pete would slip out, and her colleagues would freeze and look at her with shock, as if she had just mooned them or told a racist joke.

Cassidy spun the ring on her finger, the gems dull in the darkness. She realized how pathetic she must look: sitting here in her dead lover's sweatshirt, wearing the ring he had designed for her but would never caress again. She drained her beer, her fingers shaking.

"Thanks," she managed.

Bruce had stopped eating, and Cassidy had too. It had tasted good, but her appetite was gone.

He took their plates down to the galley, then returned and stopped at the small bar to pour two glasses of something from a squatty amber bottle. He added ice and returned to the table, placing the glass in front of her.

Cassidy managed a slight nod in thanks. They toasted, and she sipped her drink, the burn of good whiskey sliding down her throat.

"So I take it nobody showed up at the gas station?" he asked.

"No," she said, thankful for the shift in subject, purposeful or not. "But I may have figured out something else," she added.

Bruce sipped his drink, watching her curiously.

"Benita found out that Reeve paid something called Tikvah International the day you guys left Costa Rica."

"What's Tikvah International?"

Cassidy paused, swirled her drink, knowing that enjoying it too much was dangerous for her. "Remember that synagogue we passed, Chabad House?"

"Yeah."

"Well, I went in."

Bruce frowned. "Why?"

She told Bruce about being spooked by the arguing men. "I'd seen tourists go in while I was watching the Uno," she continued, sucking on an ice cube before crunching it. "Inside, tourists were having this banquette-style meal. And they were like, 'Come on in! Have some latkes!' "

Bruce gave her a look. "And did you?"

"No," she said. "But there was a poster on the wall. One of those you see in bus stations or public bathrooms." Cassidy shuddered, remembering the little boy's haunting eyes. "It was a campaign against sex trafficking. The logo on the bottom was Tikvah International's."

He wiped his mouth and set his napkin down. "The one Reeve paid before leaving Costa Rica. And . . . it's some kind of charity?" He shook his head, as if confused.

Cassidy sat back, trying to put the facts together, but there were too many holes.

"Why would Reeve pay them?" Bruce asked.

"I'm not sure." Cassidy sighed.

"Could he be mixed up in the trafficking somehow?" Bruce crossed his arms. A dark look passed over his face. "Talk about stupid," he muttered.

"What do you mean?"

Bruce got up and paced to the back of the boat. He leaned on the gunnels and gazed out over the black water. Above, the stars dusted the inky dome of sky in patterns she would never see in Eugene: belts of powdery bits of light, bright constellations, their patterns clearly visible, the Milky Way.

She crossed the distance to the gunnels, and he turned to her.

"The people who deal in human trafficking have entire armies, guns . . . there are complete patches of jungle that they have claimed as their territory." He grimaced. "They're very powerful. And ruthless. If he crossed them somehow . . . "

"So maybe that's it, then," Cassidy said, though it still didn't all fit together. "Or maybe the two aren't related at all. Maybe he did try to sell drugs, and something went wrong. Meanwhile he pays two grand to an anti-sex trafficking organization. Maybe out of guilt?"

Bruce had turned his back to the bay and was half-sitting on the gunnels, his long legs stretched out. "Maybe," he said, though he didn't sound convinced.

"Did you follow the car that chased us?" she asked.

"Yeah," he replied. "They staked out the Pelican for a while, then headed out of town. I followed as far as I could."

Cassidy shuddered at the idea of the thugs waiting for her at the hotel. "Are Benita and the others safe?" she asked. "Should we warn them?"

Bruce shook his head. "They're safe."

He sounded confident, so she told herself to believe him. "Who do you think they were?"

Bruce looked away. "Not sure."

The alcohol was starting to have the desired effect, and she swung her legs over the side of the boat, letting them dangle over the water.

"Could they be the police, and they wanted to keep what happened to Reeve quiet?" she asked.

"It's possible," Bruce said. "Nicaragua's police are sort of a joke. I mean, they keep things pleasant for the tourists, but they're paid off by big crime, and sometimes, they even run the show."

"Well, whoever it was, I received their message loud and clear." Cassidy had already come to this conclusion, but it felt good to say it out loud. "Someone doesn't want me to find out the truth."

NINETEEN

"AND YOU'RE fine leaving it at that?" Bruce asked, scrutinizing her with an intense gaze.

The desperation she felt while being chased returned with a force that made her shudder. If they'd caught her, what would they have done to her?

"I don't see any other option."

Bruce swung his legs over the gunnels to sit beside her. "I was really worried when I got to the boat and didn't find you," he said quietly.

"I'm sorry. I didn't think. I just acted. I should have tried to let you know somehow that I'd gone back."

When she and Pete were apart, they had a standing agreement to check in with each other at 8:00 p.m., either by WhatsApp if she was in Central America, or he was in Canada or Spain or Timbuktu, or by text or phone if they were stateside. After being on her own for over a year, she realized that this practice of being accountable had once again become foreign to her. Even her postdoc position was unstructured—nobody checked to see if she had made it home from the airport, or scolded her for working too late into the night. The faculty overseeing her position just expected her results and collaboration when requested. It was the way she had lived before Pete.

She and Quinn did this for each other, of course, but it was looser, and they didn't share the details of their lives the way she and Pete had.

"What'll you do, after this?" he asked.

Cassidy gazed up at the sky. How could the stars be light years away but look so close? Like they were about to fall down right on top of them. "Well, I'll probably need to call Pamela, Reeve's mom, and Rebecca, his sister, will insist that I come for a visit, which I'll refuse."

"Why?"

Cassidy huffed. "Why should I go see her? Reeve is *her* brother. She sent me on this crazy mission. She can come see me."

"Sounds like you two aren't exactly close."

"That's right. Plus, I'm going to be too busy to go anywhere for a while."

"Doing what?"

"Huh? Oh, predicting the size of Arenal's next eruption. Calculating potential lahar flow rates, coauthoring about six papers, and publishing like crazy."

He whistled. "You can do all of that?"

"I'm going to try."

"What will you tell Reeve's mom?"

"Everything," Cassidy sighed. Then, seeing Bruce's look, she added, "It's not like she doesn't know every deceitful thing he's done. The drugs, his criminal activities, his rehab . . . she'll see it for what it is."

"And that is?"

"That he got caught up in something bigger than he could handle, and it cost him his life."

Bruce was silent. They sat there as the quiet stretched between them. Cassidy listened to the water lap the sides of the boat. A breeze from the land brushed her cheek. She tucked a stray strand of hair behind her ears. It was still damp at the back of her neck. With a swift twist, she tied it up into a messy knot, allowing the cool breeze to grace her skin.

"Will those men who chased us . . . " Her heart raced at the memory. "I know you said we're safe here, but . . . are you sure?"

"You're safe," he said, his eyes locking with hers.

"After this. After I'm gone. You'll be okay, right? They won't cause trouble for you, will they?"

"Nah," Bruce said, swinging his legs back over the gunnels. "C'mon. I want to show you something."

───

"SO I SAID TO HIM, sir, please keep your pecker in your pants," Bruce finished with a cackle.

Cassidy spluttered in laughter, rolling around on the deck chair cushions they had laid out on the roof of the wheelhouse. Above them, the stars and a half moon lit the night. Bruce had been entertaining her with "the worst guest" stories, and her stomach hurt from laughing. With her mission over, and the idea of returning home starting to crystalize in her mind, a big, black cloud was forming on her horizon. Home meant the house without Pete, the solitary late nights, and the geology colleagues with their pitying looks.

Fighting it with whiskey and stories seemed as good a remedy as anything.

"Your turn," Bruce said, sipping from his drink.

"What do you mean?" she said. "I don't have any stories like that!"

"C'mon, tell me a story about a volcano erupting, or a scandal in your program. Maybe something you did?"

"Me? I'm a nerd. I've never caused a scandal."

"Never cheated on a test?"

"Never."

"Never slept with a professor?"

Cassidy laughed. "Oh, yes, I swoon for flannel and Birkenstocks. I can't keep my hands off them."

"A student?"

"Stop!" She punched his arm. "They're babies, Bruce! They can't read a map. They can't draw. They party like rock stars. They don't give two craps about the work." She sighed and took a sip of her drink. "Wait! I have a story! Does an accident count as a scandal?"

Bruce shrugged. "Sure."

"I've had rock chips get in kids' eyes, one time a rock hammer got impaled in a kid's foot, and then there was this kid who had a psychotic episode. It turns out he was bipolar but nobody could tell me about it because of HIPAA laws. Can you believe that?"

"How'd you know he was psychotic?"

"Because he was acting batshit crazy. I found out later that he stopped taking his meds! What if he tried to hurt himself or someone else?"

More memories unspooled. "Oh! This one time on a field trip, a student brought his girlfriend, and they made out in the back of the Motorpool van all freaking day. Another time, at field camp—geology majors have to complete a six-week mapping course, ours was in Montana--I hiked over this ridge looking for students who needed help with their maps and I found five students playing hacky sack. Naked."

"I've actually done that," Bruce said.

Cassidy guffawed. "Oh jeez. Please tell me why."

Bruce just shrugged. "Why not?"

Cassidy rolled her eyes. "One year, I had this one student, she was an adult, and, well, she was always kind of fragile, sort of a baby, you know, always needing help with stuff that she should know how to do, like color code a map, or how to filter her water. It was like she had never camped before. Can you imagine? A geology student who had never gone *camping*? Anyways, I had to take her to the emergency room because she refused to poop in the community bathroom or outside, and eventually she just got so backed up she *couldn't* poop."

Bruce laughed so hard he had to put down his drink.

"Oh, here's a good one," Cassidy continued, enjoying this moment of the spotlight. "This group of bikers came rumbling into town one day, and one of my students hopped on the back of a Harley and rode off into the sunset. Just like that!"

"Did she come back?" Bruce asked, alarmed.

"She was back the next morning."

"Whoa," Bruce said with a shudder. "I wouldn't hop on the back of some strange guy's motorcycle. Did she know what she was getting into?"

The mention of a motorcycle gave Cassidy an uncomfortable sensation down in her gut, but the alcohol made it feel distant, diffuse.

"I was furious," she said. "What if something had happened to her?" To her dismay, her eyes began to sting. "What if she hadn't returned? They could have left her on the side of the road somewhere. They could have hurt her," Cassidy choked out the last bit and the tears began to fall.

"Hey," Bruce said softly. "What's wrong?"

Cassidy tried to slow her breathing but her pulse was hammering against her temples. "Pete died in a motorcycle crash."

Bruce winced in empathy. "I didn't mean to bring up bad memories."

"I know," Cassidy said, furiously wiping her eyes. "It's not your fault. There's tripwires everywhere."

"I'll bet," Bruce said.

"I just...miss him," Cassidy said, and a fresh set of tears bloomed. In two days, she would be back in her house, in her big, empty bed.

Bruce was quiet, but it wasn't uncomfortable.

Cassidy closed her eyes, trying to stay in the moment. *This* moment and not in the past. Not wishing for what was gone. And not wishing that Bruce would try to make it okay. It wasn't okay. No one could make it okay—she had to the do the hard work of pushing through the grief. Alone.

"I don't want to go home," she growled, resisting the cloud of pain hovering on her horizon that would descend on her in Eugene. "It's harder." She tried to focus on the warmth of Bruce's body near hers. Would he hold her if she asked? *Stop*, a voice inside her head blared. *You've shared enough.*

With effort, she rolled away and reached for the whiskey bottle to drown her growing unease.

TWENTY

CASSIDY STIRRED and opened her eyes to pitch dark and a cool breeze coming from the land.

When she tried to swallow, her tongue felt too big for her mouth. She scanned the roof for Bruce, but she was alone. Raised voices came from below, then Bruce's rose clearly, as if in anger.

Cassidy lay still, trying to use all of her senses to understand what was happening.

A foreign voice answered in a low tone.

Her skin prickled. Someone else was on the boat.

The voices were coming from below her, on the stern. Cassidy slid to the edge and peered over the wheelhouse roof, but the deck below was covered, so Bruce and whoever was with him were hidden from view. A small outboard motorboat was tied up to the *Trinity's* starboard side.

A man laughed, but it wasn't friendly.

Cassidy rolled away from the edge, her heart hammering into her throat. Who was here?

She looked around, but the only lights shining came from the masts of the other boats. No people moved about that she could see. It was also deathly quiet except for Bruce's and the intruders' voices. Was Bruce in trouble? Should she signal for help somehow? The wheelhouse had a radio. Should she try to get to it?

The argument continued. The boat rocked and feet scuffled below her on the deck. This time she caught the tail end of Bruce's reply: " . . . *debo nada. Ya no!*"

Not anymore. What did that mean? Needing to know more, she descended the ladder past Bruce's wheelhouse and down into the galley. She crept to the other side where it opened to the stern deck.

More angry voices. Now at eye level with their feet, she couldn't make out their words.

A set of feet moved toward the galley. Did they know she was here? With a rush of panic, she realized how exposed she was.

In a flash, Cassidy was inside Jesus's room. She flattened herself against the wall behind the door, willing her heaving breaths to calm. But the intruder's feet stopped advancing.

A sickening *smack*—the noise a fist makes against flesh—sounded through the galley.

Bruce roared and there were more hits, grunts. Something thumped against the deck and slid.

Grimacing, she risked a peek from behind the door, and through the hatch, saw Bruce tumble and crash to the floor then scramble to his feet again.

A gun lay abandoned halfway between the galley hatch and where Bruce was battling two men. A trickle of sweat rolled down her temple—was the gun Bruce's?

Bruce made a lunge for the gun, but one of the men grabbed his shirt and pulled him back.

She glanced around the tiny room for a place to hide, but there was no closet—and no escape. The window above the bed was only a vent with slats. Using all the Zen she could conjure, she remained still, barely breathing, searching with her eyes for a way out. She tried to focus on the soft cotton of the hoody against her cheek and the idea that it was like her armor, a shell of protection. Her gaze went back to the bed and the space below it. She had seen the cupboard door before, but she hadn't felt comfortable poking around in Jesus's drawers. Something about that possibility sent ideas thrumming through her mind, but then shouts broke out on the deck again, followed by heavy breathing and grunts. One of the intruders yelled something she couldn't hear, but Bruce's reply came through loud and clear.

"*Tendrás que matarme.*"

You will have to kill me.

Panic exploded inside her. Lose another person she cared about? No, no, no.

In a flash, she left Jesus's room and climbed the stairs to the deck. It took a moment for the men to realize her presence, but by then she had the gun in her hands.

Bruce sat crumpled against the gunnels, as if he had just been thrown there.

"Cassidy, no!" Bruce croaked.

The two intruders loomed over him, breathing hard.

Bruce's shirt was ripped at the shoulder. His lip was bleeding, and one eye looked swollen. She wondered what other wounds lay hidden.

The intruder nearest Bruce was frozen in place and looking at her shrewdly, like a cat eyeing a mouse he was considering eating.

"Get back!" she said, pointing the gun at him. Were her hands shaking? She forced them to steady, knowing she couldn't appear weak or frightened.

The two intruders locked eyes.

Cassidy took a step forward. "*Dónde está Reeve?*"

The first man's dark face clouded with confusion. The two intruders glanced at each other.

A strange feeling settled in her chest. "*Mi hermano, dónde está?*"

The first man rattled off something in Spanish to the other one. "We don't know your brother," he replied to Cassidy in heavily accented English, then moved forward, his hand open. "Give me the gun."

Cassidy chambered a round.

"Aiee!" the man said, putting up his hands. "Don't shoot!"

"Where's Reeve! What have you done with him?" The words tumbled loose, full of hurt, and anger, but it was like someone else was speaking.

"Cassidy," Bruce said. "Put the gun down. You don't want this."

"I want the truth!" she cried. Her hand was beginning to shake, but she forced herself to be strong. Bruce was right—she did not want this, any of it. Her resolve faltered. Then she thought of Reeve, gone, probably by the hands of these very men.

"We go," the first man said, looking at Bruce. "*Pero esto no ha terminado*," he added, wiping blood off his face. *But this isn't over.*

Cassidy risked a glance at Bruce but his face was set in a hard glare.

And then the men were gone.

"Wait!" Cassidy cried, racing to the edge of the boat. Bruce grabbed her in a bear hug from behind and yanked her back. Cassidy struggled—why wasn't he letting her go after them? She wanted them to tell her what had happened, once and for all. No more playing detective, no more not knowing the answer. "Let me go!" she said, but her efforts were weak.

Bruce held her firmly, but without hurting her. "Let them go," he said softly.

What little remained of Cassidy strength drained out of her.

His fingers wrapped around hers. "Give me the gun," he coaxed.

Releasing the weapon was easy, and she did so with a sigh that morphed into a series of sobs. She folded into his arms and sighed a great, shuddering breath. Her knees began to wobble.

"Easy, there," Bruce said, and gently shifted her to the bench. He tucked the gun into his waistband. Was it his, or did it belong to the intruders? Had he been carrying it all along?

Cassidy shook from the adrenaline ebbing from her limbs.

"That was a really stupid thing to do, Cass," Bruce said finally.

"You're welcome," Cassidy said, even though his use of her nickname sent a pulse of warmth through her.

Bruce sighed again and lowered himself to the bench beside her, emitting a groan of pain. "Where in the heck did you learn to hold a gun like that?"

"Gun safety training," Cassidy replied. "Standard operating procedure for fieldwork in bear country. Plus, I grew up in Idaho. Every kid there knows how to hold a gun."

"Okay, I'm officially scared of you now," he said.

Cassidy looked over. His face was bruised and swollen. Blood was congealing on his split lip. One leg was extended, as if bending it to match the other was too painful.

"I thought you said I'd be safe on the boat," Cassidy said, wiping her face with the heels of her hands.

Bruce grimaced. "I never thought they'd trace you."

"They were after me?"

"I think it's time we get you out of here," he said instead of answering her.

The image of her empty house with the weed-riddled yard, shiny wooden floors, and the brand-new couch where she would sit, alone, hovered at the edge of her thoughts.

Bruce stood up, his face twisting in pain at the movement, and held out his hand for her to take.

"Wait, you mean, like, right *now*—like, you're going to drive the *Trinity* back, for me?"

"Yep."

"What about Benita and the other guests? And Jesus?"

"I'll be a little late coming back, but I think they won't mind. And Jesus will be thrilled to have a few extra hours with his family. I think he only took the job for a free ride to visit them."

A part of her longed to spend more time with Benita and her crew. Their friendship was an unexpected gift. And rare.

"Would you...tell the group goodbye for me?" she asked, letting him pull her to her feet.

"Of course," Bruce said with a kind smile.

Cassidy cringed when she realized what a close shave tonight had been. "Would they really have . . . killed you?"

"The important part is you're safe now. Let's keep it that way."

A pulse of gratitude washed through her, making her knees wobble. "Okay, but do we need to get you to a hospital first? You don't look so good."

"Nope," Bruce said, trying to smile, then stopped when his lip started bleeding again. "I've been in worse shape."

Cassidy gave him a shrewd once-over. "Okay, then at least let me take care of readying the boat."

Bruce gave her a tight nod, and headed for the wheelhouse.

Once below deck, Cassidy made sure to lock every latch on the kitchen drawers, to secure the fridge door, and put away their dinner dishes and the items remaining on the counter.

Jesus's door was still open, and she hurried to close it as the sound of the anchor winch whirring to life filled the cabin.

With her hand on the doorknob, the same tickle in her brain from earlier returned. Drawn in by a feeling she couldn't ignore anymore, Cassidy knelt down at the small door beneath Jesus's bed. Carefully, she turned the latch and looked inside.

"Bruce!" she cried.

TWENTY-ONE

BRUCE LIMPED INTO THE CABIN, gun in hand at his side, his quick gaze first scanning her surroundings before connecting with hers.

"What's wrong?" he said, grimacing as he limped the rest of the way into the cabin.

"Sorry," Cassidy said quickly. "I didn't mean to alarm you."

With a questioning look at her, Bruce tucked his gun into the back of his waistband.

Cassidy pointed at the open cupboard space. "I think I just figured out something. Reeve had someone on this boat. In here."

"What?" Bruce blinked. "Some *one?*"

The facts had been in front of her all along. She had just interpreted them wrong. From Reeve's partying apartment neighbor and the young girl he was with, to the payment Reeve made, to the "delivery." She begged Reeve to forgive her for being so blind. *I've been wrong from the very beginning,* she thought. *I'm so sorry.*

It had to be the answer to Reeve's disappearance. He had paid Tikvah International to rescue the woman in the picture. His girlfriend, Jade. Then smuggled her aboard the *Trinity* to San Juan and delivered her to safety.

After a week of searching for answers, of wondering, of suffering through many ugly imaginings about Reeve's fate, she finally had the answer.

"Jade. His girlfriend. He hid her in here during the trip and brought her ashore to rescue her." Cassidy peered into the space, which contained a jumble of life vests, a bilge pump, and emergency rations.

The look on Reeve's face in the picture that day on the beach said it all: triumph.

"*In there?*" Bruce said, and Cassidy could almost see the gears turning in his mind.

Cassidy nodded. "It's the only thing that makes sense. Whenever he could, he would stay on the boat, remember? That was when he could let her out."

Bruce rubbed his jaw, doubtful. "You said rescue . . . "

"I don't know for sure, but I think she was a prostitute, an illegal one. Why else would he risk bringing her here? Someone must have owned her, and he was taking her away from him." Cassidy remembered the man in the shadows outside Reeve's apartment. He had been waiting for the young *chica*, to finish her job so he could deliver her to the next customer in line. Cassidy wanted to cry out in anguish. Why hadn't she grabbed the girl and run? Why hadn't she done something to help her?

"There's no way," Bruce said, standing. "I would have known she was down there."

"You sure? She was probably a master at being silent. She knew what was at stake. Reeve had bought her a ticket out of a life of slavery, and she was on her way to being free."

"Damn," Bruce whispered, crossing his arms. He turned away from her.

She gave him a minute to process her discovery. "It was you who actually gave me the idea. Remember what you said about Jesus only taking the job to get a free ride? Well, that was sort of what Reeve was doing, only the free ride was for Jade."

Bruce glanced at her, his features sharp. "So then what happened?"

"He had paid Tikvah International the day before the trip. So after he brought Jade ashore, he delivered her to them, to safety." Or at least that's what she hoped. "After that, I don't know."

Pete had investigated a story once on a sex trafficking ring in Sicily, but had to give up because of lack of sources. He had tried to shield her from the gruesome details, but she had learned them anyway. It was still incomprehensible to her that people would steal or buy a human being and sell her or him into a life filled with such horror. Like a commodity, or an animal.

"Maybe he was the victim of some kind of revenge, or maybe he just ran into some bad luck." She paused, the guilt of not taking Reeve's call those many weeks ago hitting her like an icy wave. What if that phone call had been his last? What if she had been his final hope?

"I don't think we'll ever know," she said, bracing herself against the wall.

He glanced at her. "So what did he do with all the stuff I store under his bunk while his girlfriend was in there?"

Cassidy shook her head. "Reeve can be pretty creative when he wants to be."

Bruce stood. "After that trip, we had a rat problem. I couldn't figure it out," he said, starting to pace. "I'll bet they ate in here. She may even have kept food under there. I can't believe this happened, and I didn't even know about it."

He gave a groan and turned to go. "He could have screwed this whole thing up," he muttered, then limped from the cabin.

Cassidy joined Bruce in preparing for departure, helping him stow loose items in the galley, locking cupboards, closing the doors on the guests' cabins. Sooner than she expected, the *Trinity's* big engines rumbled to life, and then they were accelerating out of the calm waters of the bay. Cassidy stood on the stern deck, her eyes fixed on the mountains behind San Juan del Sur, a black cutout against the bright stars. She glanced up to the wheelhouse where Bruce steered toward open water, his back to her. A surge of emotions swirled inside her: relief, gratitude, sorrow.

As the *Trinity* rounded the point and the lights of the town blinked out of sight, Cassidy climbed to the wheelhouse.

"It's a good thing we're doing this," Bruce said, his broken face tight with worry. "You're in more danger than I thought."

CASSIDY WOKE in Bruce's bed. A pale light outlined the curve of land to the east and as she watched, the green and gray hilltops softened with a buttery glow. Around them, the water extended in all directions like a sheet of shiny, blue-black glass.

Bruce glanced back at her from the helm. "Buenas días, *dormilona*." He grinned, but it was lopsided, half of his face swollen and bruised, and his lip fat and scabbed. He must have cleaned himself up in the night because he sported a fresh T-shirt and his cheeks were no longer bloody.

"Stop calling me that," Cassidy grumbled, though without malice. She had woken several times in the night, but had kept quiet, choosing to let the motor's rumble and Bruce's quiet presence deliver her back to sleep.

Bruce turned back to the helm. "There's some coffee left," he said, indicating a thermos sitting upright in a holder in the nav station. "No donuts today, though, sorry."

"You're fired," Cassidy said with a yawn. She pushed herself to a sitting position.

Bruce laughed, then sucked in a grimace.

"Sorry," she said, coming to stand next to him. "Ribs?"

He nodded. "At least it's not my kidneys," he answered.

She poured a cup of coffee into the thermos's lid and took a sip. After a few more, her headache began to ebb.

"We'll be in Playas del Coco in about a half hour. From there you can hop a bus to Liberia. There's a weekday ten a.m. flight to Houston."

Cassidy finished her coffee. "I have to go back to Tamarindo, first," she said, replacing the lid on the thermos.

She sensed Bruce stiffen.

"What?" She glanced at him. "I can't leave without my laptop, my field gear."

He swallowed. "Of course," he replied. "There's probably another flight later. I think Delta has one in the afternoon, through Dallas."

"You have them all memorized?"

He grinned. "I'm not only the captain, surf guide, and book-keeper. I'm also the chauffeur."

Cassidy watched the barren hillsides and hidden coves pass. The cool morning air felt fresh and clean. She felt the shift inside her, a bubble of optimism forming—as if the events in San Juan were farther into her past than just a few hours.

After gathering her remaining things, she went to the bow to sit alone while Bruce piloted the boat into Playas del Coco's tranquil bay, the big engines slowing. The constant *shusssh* of water calving around the boat seemed extra loud in the still morning air, and she imagined all the chores that the townspeople were waking up to: start the cooking fire, feed the animals, make rice, get ready for school or work. Her own list of chores was waiting, too, back in the States.

The boat slowed again, and the town's buildings sharpened into focus. She spotted the hotel where she had started her journey with Bruce, its white wrap-around porch glowing bright in the dawn's silvery light.

A small skiff left the shore and headed straight for them. Soon it was idling next to the *Trinity*, with Bruce rattling off instructions to the boy at the helm. And then it was time to say goodbye.

"Sorry for all of this," she said.

"Sorry for what? Caring about your brother?"

She studied his battered face. He was still handsome, maybe more so. "Thanks for bringing me back."

"Thanks for saving my life," Bruce replied, taking her hand. He closed his eyes and gave her palm a soft squeeze. She took that moment to study him, to imprint him in her mind. When he opened his eyes and saw her watching, he leaned down and kissed her softly on the cheek. A nervous tingle shivered over her skin, but she held still and savored his kindness. Leaving him now felt strange. Would she ever see him again?

He pulled away, and a shadow crossed his eyes. "Be careful, Cassidy, okay?"

She frowned. Hadn't they left the danger behind them in Nicaragua?

With that, Bruce stepped back to let Cassidy climb into the skiff. As the boy steered the boat towards the shore, and Cassidy risked a look back. Instead of the warm smile she expected, Bruce's eyes were dark with worry.

TWENTY-TWO

ARRIVING in Tamarindo after a hot taxi ride, she stopped at a beachside café for breakfast. It felt unnerving to eat alone; since her arrival in Costa Rica she had been surrounded by the constant chatter of other diners—whether friends or fellow travelers. She savored her coffee and watched the children playing in the small waves breaking on the cocoa-colored sand, eating her beans and eggs slowly as her thoughts shifted and tumbled in her mind.

The cloud of melancholy she'd kept at bay was edging closer. The moment she stepped off the plane in the States, it would envelop her. Her grief counselor, Jay had coached her on this, suggesting she call a friend to meet her instead of tackling it alone. But she had no one in Eugene but him.

After staying for as long as she felt was polite at the restaurant, she paid her bill and strolled the beach to Crazy Mike's.

Cassidy walked the cold sand, empty of vacationers this early, but the lineup was dotted with surfers. Macho stood giving a lesson to a group of young women in bikinis. He gave her a wink as she passed by, and she smiled to herself, content to know that Pura Vida was alive and well.

Inside the restaurant, Mel wasn't behind the bar. Cassidy felt disoriented, as if him being gone signified that she might have stepped into the wrong wrinkle in time. Indeed, the whole restaurant felt different without him at the center of it. She continued to the small counter near the board cage where a clipboard showed guests' names and room numbers.

"Welcome back," Aliana said from behind the counter, her smile bright.

"Morning," Cassidy replied. "Would you do me a huge favor?"

Aliana listened to Cassidy's request to call the airlines, then immediately picked up the phone. Cassidy waited while Aliana bantered with the agent on the other end for several minutes. When Aliana hung up, she gave Cassidy a triumphant grin. "I was able to get you on tomorrow morning's flight. Ten a.m."

Cassidy had been banking on the afternoon flight, like Bruce had suggested.

"Do you have a room for tonight?" she asked, so tired that crawling into one of the beds and sleeping until dinnertime seemed like a great idea. She also needed to charge her phone and laptop so she could use the long flight home to start catching up on her substantial workload. With dismay she remembered that her phone charging cord was in the hotel in San Juan. Ugh. Maybe she could find a sympathetic guest who could loan her one for a few hours.

Aliana's smile crumpled into a sorrowful frown. "I'm so sorry, but we are booked."

Cassidy tried to hide her grimace. "Do you have a recommendation?"

"Of course," Aliana said, and returned to the phone.

After a series of calls, Cassidy was booked at Casa Pacifica, with her airport shuttle arranged as well.

"But check-in there is not until four o'clock," Aliana warned. "You are welcome to use our pool and restaurant until then. We also have very comfortable hammocks," she added with a wink.

. . .

WHILE WORKING, she consumed a gallon of coffee plus an entire plate of fluffy pancakes with butter and syrup. There were only two outlets in the restaurant, and though she lurked, the tables near them remained occupied, and by mid-afternoon Cassidy's laptop's battery was long dead, as was her phone. So she edited the hard copy of her upcoming submission, a piece for *Nature Geoscience* about the correlation between the number of harmonics in a tremor signal and eruption intensity. After, she enjoyed one last dip in the pool and used the outdoor shower to rinse off and ready her mind for her final night in Tamarindo.

Every now and then she looked towards the bar, expecting to see Mel, but he never showed. She considered asking one of the staff about his whereabouts, but then thought better of it. A strange tug of war was taking place inside her mind. Her night with Mel seemed so far in the past compared to what she had experienced in San Juan.

Images of Bruce and what they had been through had revisited her throughout the day, and the strange feeling she had experienced while saying goodbye wouldn't leave her alone.

Finally, unable to resist the pull of a soft bed and quiet, she paid her bill and packed up her things. After a last look around the restaurant and the pool, the scraggly trees with their yellow trumpet-shaped blossoms and the beautiful beach, she turned away and walked out into the street.

The temperature on the road felt several degrees hotter than in the breeze-cooled restaurant, and her skin beaded with sweat from every pore within seconds. Insects buzzed from the roadside bushes as she trudged past. Aliana had given her directions—Casa Pacifico was back from the beach a few blocks, more towards the center of town.

Two Tico boys on bikes passed her, chattering loudly, and she thought of Macho, Eddie, and Rico, and her death-defying ride on the handlebars.

She turned up a street and hiked away from the beach, through a residential area. Small houses engulfed by jungle foliage lined the dirt road. Her backpack was beginning to feel heavy; there was some-thing poking into her left kidney.

Cassidy jiggled her pack, trying to shift whatever it was, but with no luck. At the next intersection, she paused, double-checking her directions, then turned left and walked some more. The hotel should be appearing soon. She had come to a row of apartments, flanked by empty jungle, and houses with corrugated tin roofs. One appeared to be a makeshift restaurant; a woman wearing a faded flower-print apron tended a wood stove beneath a flat iron surface sizzling with cooking meat. She did not look up at Cassidy's passing.

After another block of walking, Cassidy recognized Reeve's apartment building. In the daytime, the surrounding area lacked the menacing shadows and shifty activity as her last visit. She walked to the entrance and paused, wondering if her feet had brought her here on purpose.

She had been thinking about the girl who had disappeared into the neighbor's apartment, and the man waiting for her return outside. How did such a system even work? Had the neighbor called a secret phone number, and ordered up his request? *I'll take a thin one with long hair who looks terrified, age fourteen or fifteen, and make it snappy.* Or was there a website, like Benita had said, and a customer need only click? The concept made her blood boil. The system should be destroyed. How could people do such terrible things to children?

As if drawn by some invisible force, Cassidy entered the build-ing. Climbing the narrow stairs, she thought about Reeve walking these same steps, imagined him leading Jade by the hand down the hallway. The stained and dingy walls didn't look any more cheery in the daytime. From one of the rooms came the thumping sounds of vigorous drumming, presumably from a set of bongos.

Reaching the end of the hall, Cassidy noticed that Reeve's door-knob had been fixed. Someone had likely taken over his space. What had they done with Reeve's broken things? Thrown them into the street? Hauled them off to some pile in the jungle? She paused, wondering what to do, then remembered the neighbor. She stepped to his door and gave it a knock. A feeling of intense rage surfaced, and she hit the door again, harder, until she was pounding with her fist.

A middle-aged man with ebony skin emerged from the door halfway down the hall. "Hey!" he called out in Caribbean-accented English. "You tryin' to bring down dis door?"

Cassidy paused, her knuckles throbbing. She shook her head. "No," she said, her small voice barely a whisper. *Just this apartment.*

The man's dreadlocks did not stir when he shook his head. "He gone," the man said. "The police take him away."

Cassidy watched him curiously. "Why?"

"Too many parties. People coming and going at all hours of de day and night."

Cassidy frowned. She did not know what he meant, but felt somehow that she should.

"It bettah now. Much more quiet." His wrinkled face calmed.

Cassidy lowered her arm from the neighbor's doorway and shuffled down the hall, sensing the man's eyes on her as she passed.

"Did Peter send you?" he asked.

For a moment, it was like he the floor has vanished and she was falling slowly through space. "What?" she asked, gulping for air.

The man gave an impatient stomp of his foot. "Did you evah meet him?"

Cassidy shook her head to clear what she had clearly misheard. Of course, Pete did not send her here. In fact, if Pete was alive, wouldn't he have warned her not to come?

"Yes," Cassidy said, slowly recovering her composure. "I was looking for someone else, and he . . . came. He had a girl with him," she added, unable to ban the image of the two together.

"He no good," the dreadlocked man said, his voice somber.

"I wanted . . . " Cassidy stopped. Why was she telling this to a stranger? It didn't matter now.

Shaking his head, the man closed the door.

Outside the apartment building, Cassidy took great, heaping

lungfuls of air—as if she had just surfaced from a deep dive. She popped the waist belt of the backpack. It slid off her shoulders and landed softly in the dirt, the hip belt curving up like the limbs of a dead insect. She leaned on her knees, gasping, and the tears dripped down, making dark spots in the dirt. She sank to her pack and wept.

TWENTY-THREE

CASSIDY TURNED ANOTHER CORNER, knowing she was lost, but not able to arrive at a plan that would get her found. Her brain was working by instinct, and she just walked—first to get away, and after because she didn't know how to stop.

Her grief counselor had encouraged her to walk or ride a bike to process her emotions, but it always sounded hokey, as if a stroll through the park would get her out of her head.

A "walk" was a waste of time, but she found a vigorous hike or an adrenaline-packed mountain bike ride could be helpful, even if only for a little while.

But walking here in Tamarindo was not helping, with the sun closing on the horizon and her hotel hidden somewhere in this maze.

The man with dreadlocks asking, "Did Peter send you?" rang in her head. She allowed herself a very short fantasy of Pete here beside her, hiking along, brainstorming answers to the holes in Reeve's story. He would be asking her questions, examining every tidbit of information from each angle. She was sure he would insist on finding Reeve's grave. Pete never gave up.

Had she given up on Reeve? Regret threatened to bring the curtain down on her again, but she pushed it away.

"No!" she said, her voice garbled by her clenched teeth.

"Cassidy?" a voice called.

Cassidy stopped in her tracks and searched the darkening street for the source. Was she hearing things now?

She stood near a small market, the kind attached to someone's home which was so common in rural parts of Latin America. A jeep stood parked outside.

About to slide into the driver's side seat of the jeep stood Mel.

A rush of relief so powerful overcame her that her chest hollowed, sending a powerful ache into her shoulders. Mel met her halfway in the muddy street.

"What the hell are you doing out here?" he said, his cornflower-blue eyes looking her up and down, as if the answer to his question could be found there.

"I'm looking for my hotel," she answered.

Mel looked around, incredulous. "Here?"

"I . . . got lost," she said, though as soon as she did, wished she could take it back. She was not the kind of woman who got lost. Ever.

"What hotel?" he asked, slipping her backpack off her shoulders and carrying it to the jeep.

"Casa Pacifica," she said, surprised the name hadn't deserted her. "Can you take me?"

"Of course," he said. "Hop in."

Cassidy slid into the passenger seat, buckled the chunky, old-school seat belt, and then felt silly when Mel didn't use his. Mel pulled the jeep in a U-turn, its knobby tires humming over the thick mud. He reached into the backseat and put something cold into her hands: a bottle of chilled water.

Cassidy gave him a look of gratitude, and he winked.

"I didn't know you were back," he said, pressing the off button on his phone, which was held by two prongs mounted on the dashboard.

A flicker of guilt sank into her gut. "Yeah, I . . . got in this morning." She glanced at him. "I looked for you," she added, as if sharing this would make up for the way she had neglected him.

"I was out of town, checking out some property," he said, then flashed her a smile.

Cassidy watched the verdant green leaves and canopy flash by and cracked the lid of her bottle of water. The icy water lowered her anxiety another notch.

They passed a group of tourists and a fancy-looking restaurant with a line of people waiting to get in.

"When you texted me last, you were heading out to where Reeve's phone was found," Mel said. "Did you find anything?" he asked, his eyes squinting in that way people do when expecting difficult news.

The idea of explaining everything suddenly overwhelmed her. "No," she managed, which of course wasn't true. Yet it was. She had little proof that Reeve had been killed, but it was the only explanation that fit, given what she'd learned about Tikvah International and the photo of Reeve with the girl. Jade.

Unable to push the exhaustion out of her voice, she replied, "Uh, it's been kind of a long day."

"How was the rest of the trip?" he probed. "Good waves?"

"Yeah," Cassidy said. She wondered when her ability to carry on a conversation would return. Maybe after drinking this water.

"Bruce took good care of me," she added—then realized her mistake. "I mean us," she corrected quickly, though it made her feel weird. "And the food was amazing. Everything was really great."

"Well," Mel said, giving her a long, careful look. "I'm glad you're back safe." He downshifted the gears, and the jeep descended a winding road.

They neared the center of town, giving her occasional glimpses of the ocean between the restaurants and hotels. The sun was melting a red stain into the sea, the sky above changing by the second: first pink, then orange, and now stripes of white and yellow over a backdrop of a bright magenta. It felt like a special gift on her last night in town, and she took a moment to savor it.

"There's a rumor that Bruce isn't all that he seems, so I'm glad to hear it's not true," Mel said as they approached an intersection.

Cassidy choked on a gulp of cold water. "What do you mean?" she managed.

Mel sighed. "Nah, forget it. He's a good guy. I never believed it anyways."

"Okay, really," she said, turning in her seat. "Now you have to tell me."

Mel paused, looking both ways at the intersection before crossing, the jeep accelerating. She could smell the sea now, mingling with the aroma of grilling food.

"I'm a bartender, so, you know, people tell me all kinds of garbage." He chuckled a little. "But I heard that he supplements his income with smuggling. You know, that boat of his."

Cassidy caught his casual look, and sat back, thinking: *Bruce, a smuggler?* "Like, drugs?"

Mel shrugged. "I guess. I have no idea."

"Stop," Cassidy said. "Stop the car."

Alarmed, Mel eased the jeep off to the side of the road. They were in a busy section of the town, with pedestrians moving along the broken sidewalk in a steady stream. It felt claustrophobic, like there wasn't enough space in the town—or the world—for her.

"Why are there so many people here?" she said, her voice sounding desperate.

"Because it's Thanksgiving," he replied.

"It is?" Cassidy replied, feeling even more off-kilter. "Today?"

"No, it's Tuesday today. Thanksgiving isn't until Thursday."

Cassidy was so annoyed at herself for needing to ask such a stupid question that she swung her legs out of the cab and strode off toward the beach.

A sense of overwhelm thundered through her hard enough to

block the sound of the waves and the tourists on the street, leaving her only with the fast whoosh of her breathing.

It couldn't be true about Bruce, but of course she'd been wrong before. Trusting people who only hurt her.

How could Bruce be involved with something illegal? *Wouldn't I know if Bruce was some kind of criminal?* However, little details that had bugged her were surfacing. Like the way he had jumped her on the boat. That he had a gun. What he had said to the intruders? ... *then you're going to have to kill me.*

She had assumed that he had been protecting her, but why would he die for her, a stranger? It was entirely possible that the encounter had been about something else, like a job he was doing, or refusing. Then, she remembered the envelope he had handed to the hotel owner on that first day at the hotel in Playa del Coco. What if that had been some kind of payoff?

The panic rose in her faster and faster, driven by a sense of danger, of hurt and confusion. She knew the only way to stop it was to ground herself in her surroundings.

Sights.

Smells.

Sensations.

Anything to pull her from the place of terror that was locked in the past.

She began to run down the narrow path lined with scraggly trees and ground scrub, arriving at the edge of the surf, shaking, her breaths desperate. She kicked off her sandals and hurried into the black water up to her waist. The warm water gave her a needed jolt of reality.

She let the water coat her skin, inhaled the thick salt. *I am here,* she told herself. *Not in the past, not in that black hole where the memories live.*

Mel waded toward her, his eyes tight with worry.

Cassidy dunked under the water, using the moment to fully ground herself.

I'm okay.

When she surfaced, the fear had lessened. She could breathe easier.

She wiped her wet hair back from her forehead.

"I'm all about the midnight swim, but I get the sense something's wrong," Mel said kindly.

A wave came and she bobbed over it, free-floating over the frothy tip. She took her time organizing her thoughts. What had just happened—that rising panic—was a sign that she wasn't as strong as she thought. It meant she needed support, though picking up the threads with Jay when she returned home made her stomach harden into a ball.

"It was what you said about Bruce," Cassidy said. A tremor of the panic zipped through her, but she calmed it with a deep breath.

The waves pushed and the current tugged at her legs. She wondered how difficult it would be to get swept away. *Maybe that's the answer,* she thought. *I could crawl out of the ocean in some new place and forget all about Nicaragua.*

"I found out what happened to Reeve," she added. Maybe it would be good to talk about it with someone like Mel, still mostly a stranger in many ways. "He tried to rescue a girl from the sex trade."

"Whoa," Mel said over the crash of a wave on the shore.

"But I must have triggered something, and some men came after me."

A shadow passed over Mel's face.

Cassidy bobbed over another lump of swell. "Bruce helped me escape. He even brought me back last night to make sure I was safe, so when you said he might be involved in something illegal..."

They dipped into the trough of the wave, and it feathered and broke behind them.

"Like I said, I'm sure that rumor isn't true," Mel said. "People like to talk, that's all. I shouldn't have said anything."

Cassidy wanted to believe this. Maybe someday, she could

examine the facts in greater detail, try to find the truth. But maybe it was better to leave it all behind.

AT THE HOTEL, Mel hoisted her backpack and walked her in to the small, brightly-lit lobby. A half-dozen college-aged kids milled about, talking loudly, with generous use of the F-bomb. Beyond the desk, Cassidy saw a rectangular pool, with rooms lining its edge. She counted five people in the pool, one lounging on an air mattress, and heard reggae music thumping low and steady from an invisible speaker. The layout reminded her of a motel her family used to stay at when her dad had driven them back and forth to Ventura while dating Pamela.

The panic from earlier echoed through her, a powerful reminder of her fragile state. In this place, surrounded by happy groups and pairs of people, she would feel even more isolated.

No.

Quickly, before her emotions could topple over, Cassidy turned around and walked out of the hotel.

TWENTY-FOUR

MEL CAME UP BESIDE HER, his eyes warm and kind. "Tell me what you need, darlin'."

"Somewhere quiet. Something to eat. A soft bed," she said, and it felt so good to finally find her voice, to take control.

Mel seemed to think for a moment. "I have a friend who's out of town. I'm sure he'd let you stay a night. I could call—"

The thought of being alone crashed down on her. She shook her head.

Mel gave her a thoughtful glance, as if he could read her mind. "Of course, you can stay with me," he said. "As long as you don't mind the frogs, it's quiet."

Relief flooded through her. She smiled. "I don't mind frogs."

Mel lifted her pack into the back of the jeep, then paused, his eyes sparkling. "How do you feel about treehouses?"

Cassidy laughed, and man, did it feel good, easy, making her fear from earlier feel far away. "You live in a treehouse?"

"Best view in town," he said.

She stepped close and he folded her into his arms.

"Thank you," she said.

"Don't thank me yet. I haven't been home in a few days. The geckos might have taken over the place."

If Cassidy hadn't been so hungry, she would have fallen asleep in the jeep. They stopped at a roadside restaurant where Mel had dashed inside then returned with two Styrofoam boxes. Whatever was inside them smelled divine. Mel navigated the streets, eventually turning onto a winding road that crested a hilltop. A handful of nicer homes peppered the vast jungle, sharp corners or brightly colored paint poking out of the trees, one home with a giant metal gate and guardhouse. In between were SE VENDE signs posted on trees or rusted barbed-wire fences. Even though they had only been driving for fifteen minutes, the busy town felt distant.

Mel turned down a muddy, rutted driveway lined with purple flowering trees. After a short distance, a structure that could have come from a storybook emerged. Tiny lights lined a stairway that zigzagged up to a square home in a large tree high off the ground. A covered porch wrapped around it.

"Wow," Cassidy breathed as a shiver of anticipation tingled her skin.

Mel parked at the base of the stairway and removed the takeout boxes from her lap.

Without the purr of the jeep's engine, the humming, buzzing, and chirping coming from every corner of the canopy filled her ears.

She stepped out of the jeep and grabbed her pack while Mel scooped up his grocery bags with his other hand.

"Let's go up," he said with a grin.

Cassidy shouldered her backpack and followed him up the long stairway. Once through a thick, heavily polished door with a driftwood doorknob, they stepped into a large, open space.

A small kitchen area with a wood countertop, narrow fridge, and a range filled the left corner. In the center of the room, a giant tree trunk extended through a hole in the floor and continued through the ceiling to the upper level. A set of stairs curved around the tree to what Cassidy assumed was the bedroom. At the base of the stairs was a simple futon couch with end tables crafted from gnarled hardwood. Cassidy set her pack by the couch and walked further into the room, admiring the warm feel of the wood, and the way she felt part of the forest.

The main floor extended to a covered porch that faced a vast expanse of jungle. A pair of wooden rocking chairs sat vacant with a square wooden table between them. On the table was a pair of large binoculars and a bird identification book.

Along the left wall, between the kitchen and the porch, was a small office space consisting of a narrow, roll-top desk and stool. Though it didn't look out of place here, she wondered what a bar owner needed a home office for. Maybe he did orders from home instead of staying late at Crazy Mike's.

"This is amazing," Cassidy said, savoring the airy, open feel of being high in the trees.

Mel, who was now mixing drinks at the kitchen counter, gave her a rakish grin.

Though the sun had long since set, she imagined a sweeping view over the gray-green canopy that sloped down to the shiny sea. The sunrise would be equally stunning and Cassidy imagined drinking coffee from the porch with Mel at her side.

A breeze blew softly from the ocean and she rubbed her bare arms. She realized how sticky and salty her skin felt.

"You don't happen to have a shower up here, do you?" she asked.

He raised an eyebrow. "But of course." He used a long metal stir stick from one of the drinks to point in the direction around the deck's corner. "Help yourself. Towels are in the cupboard."

Relieved, Cassidy grabbed a set of clothes from her pack and then followed the deck around the corner. A low partition made of frosted glass blocks ended in a stone wall with a simple spigot. The concrete floor sloped into a shallow bowl with a drain in the center. She stripped down and in moments, the warm, clean water slid over her skin. Above her, a screened roof had collected a handful of large leaves. She scrubbed in the vanilla-scented shampoo, knowing she was hurrying, pulled by the anticipation she'd experienced since getting into Mel's jeep.

She turned off the water and dried off with a soft, fluffy towel. She squeezed out her long hair then stepped into her clothes—nothing special—a blue T-shirt (had she slept in this one?) and pair of long hiking shorts.

When she rounded the corner, Mel sat in one of the leather-backed rocking chairs on the deck. The bird book and binoculars had been put away, and two plates, cloth napkins, and silverware were placed on the small table along with a candle and two tall cocktail glasses. Soothing Latin instrumental music played from inside.

"Thanks for doing all of this," Cassidy said, fighting a sense of overwhelm. It was her last day of vacation—why shouldn't she spend it with a handsome friend-in-the-making who seemed content to take care of her?

"It's my pleasure," Mel said.

Cassidy picked up her drink and clinked hers with his in a toast. She sipped from the drink, the ice cubes tapping against her teeth, tasting fresh mint, lime, and a hint of sweetness.

They dug into the food, some kind of Asian bowl with rice, grilled cabbage, and fish in a spicy sauce.

"How long have you been in Tamarindo?" Cassidy asked between bites.

"Coming up on fifteen years."

Cassidy took another sip of her drink, imagining the changes Mel had seen in a town like Tamarindo. Changes that were good for his business, but maybe not so great for actually enjoying his time off—more traffic, crowded lineups, unruly tourists.

Cassidy swallowed another bite and washed it down with another sip from her glass, rocking a bit in her chair. After such a taxing afternoon, to unwind in quiet company felt almost magical.

"You said you'd been out of town looking at property," Cassidy asked. "Was it for surfing?"

Mel was mid-sip, so he nodded, then smacked his lips. "A little scouting trip."

"Anything you wish to share?"

"My boat's nothing fancy," he said. "But you're welcome anytime."

Cassidy identified the subtle rub against Bruce, but out of fear that it would expose her insecurities again, didn't let thoughts of Bruce linger. Though what if his big, fancy boat was financed with dirty money, and he had fooled her?

Cassidy set her plate aside and spun the ring on her finger. When she returned home, maybe she would be brave enough to finally take it off.

Mel disappeared inside with their plates, and when he returned, he stood at the side of her chair and held out his hand.

"May I have this dance?" he asked.

A warmth filled her insides as she gazed into his bright blue eyes. Cassidy let Mel pull her to her feet. As she slipped into his arms, the painful road she had been walking dissolved into the night.

CASSIDY WOKE the way she usually did, from a haze of a dream in the middle of the night. The insects had quieted somewhat; though a breeze—coming from the land now—stirred the branches of the giant tree, making a sound like water moving over stones. The tree also seemed to be swaying gently. Maybe this movement had woken her.

Barely visible in the inky darkness, Mel was facing away from her, curled on his side, his left shoulder arching up in the darkness. She curled into his back, wrapping an arm around his waist, and tried to go back to sleep. Mel stirred but didn't wake.

Her mind turned to the day ahead: catching her shuttle to the airport, boarding her plane, and the many connections that followed. It would take the entire day to travel back to Eugene, but she would use her time to jump back into her projects.

With a start, she remembered that her laptop battery was dead. Her phone, too. She rolled to her back, surrendering to the fact that further sleep would elude her until she could plug in her electronics. After rolling carefully from the bed, she tiptoed down the stairs, gliding her hands down the trunk of the tree in the darkness to the main floor.

Even after she gave her eyes—gummy from sleeping in her contacts—a minute to adjust, it was still too dark to see. Shuffling her feet slowly, she extended her hands to catch herself if she stumbled, until her toe hit the soft nylon of her backpack propped up against the couch.

She unclipped the top and felt inside the main pouch for her padded laptop case. After removing it, she went back for her phone, finally finding it in the lid inside a special zippered pocket, along with her passport and wallet. Unfortunately, her charging cord was back at the Pelican Hotel in Nicaragua. She remembered Mel's phone mounted to the dash of the jeep—wasn't it a Samsung like hers? Maybe he had a spare cord somewhere.

Cassidy checked the wall space next to the couch, then kitchen, squinting in the dark. She found only one outlet, both sockets plugged with cords from appliances.

Then she remembered the roll-top desk. Carefully, she shuffled to the other side of the room, expecting any second to run into something that would make her fall and wake Mel. Earlier, she had seen a small lamp atop the desk but worried the light would disturb Mel, so she felt down the wall, discovering an outlet in the floor, with two plugs already in the sockets.

Relieved, she traced the cords up through a hole in the back of the desk. Cassidy paused, unsure about proceeding. Would Mel mind her opening his desk and borrowing his charging cord? She stood there in the dark, debating. If the roles were reversed, how would she feel about it? The idea of someone in the house she and Pete had shared gave her gut a lurch, but she pushed past it when the answer surfaced: of course, she wouldn't mind helping him out.

Carefully, she rolled back the lid of the desk. The thick wood squeaked once but then tucked back inside itself without further protest. A phone was plugged in, but a separate cord lay vacant—probably for a laptop. Maybe he used it at the surf camp, but only sometimes brought it home.

With a careful tug, she released the cord from his phone. As she did so, it came to life, the screen full of text messages. She ignored these, but noted the time: 3:06 a.m. Feeling more and more guilty for messing with Mel's things without permission, she went to plug in her phone when his screen lit up with an incoming call.

When the image of the caller filled the screen, Cassidy didn't believe her eyes. She should have taken the time to remove her contact lenses before falling asleep, but she had been so content, lazy almost, and hadn't wanted to disrupt the enchantment of letting sleep come leisurely, sweetly, in Mel's arms.

But the longer she stared, the harder it was to ignore what she was seeing.

It was Reeve's neighbor, the man with the young *chica*. The name JUNO flashed below his image.

Her logical brain engaged immediately, searching for a solution. Maybe Juno worked for Mel at Crazy Mike's. Like a night watchman, and something was wrong. A fire? Could someone be hurt?

However, Cassidy had never seen Juno at Crazy Mike's. Maybe the two of them were surf buddies. *That's probably it.* Maybe they were supposed to go surfing this morning, and Juno was calling to wake him up, or to change the plan.

A frisson of nerves shot through her. Only fanatical surfers got up at three a.m. Was Mel the fanatical kind?

And Juno hadn't struck her as a hardcore surfer, either, with his soft belly and tired eyes.

On full alert now, she picked up Mel's phone again. Juno's call ended without a message. She scanned the previews of the text messages, all from different no-name phone numbers. They were written in some strange code, like E36 2,200, A91 1800. Another no-name number's text message read: New photos operational.

Cassidy lowered herself to the stool to organize her thoughts. Just because Mel knew Juno didn't mean something was wrong. It was a small town. Mel was a business owner, he probably knew everyone.

However, Juno seemed shady. Why was he calling Mel at this hour? She remembered the dreadlocked drummer at the apartment. *He's a bad man. People coming and going at all hours of the day and night.*

Supposedly, he had been arrested. Had he been freed? Was that the reason for the call? To ask Mel to bail him out?

Cassidy was relieved to have found an answer. Of course, that was it. Mel was the kind of guy who would bail out a local kid in trouble.

She plugged in her phone then tried to weave her laptop cord into the hole in the back of the desk so she could plug it into the floor. That's when she noticed the camera. The message flashed into her mind: *New photos operational.* She remembered the bird book and binoculars on the deck's table. Maybe Mel was some kind of nature photographer.

A seed of doubt crept into her mind. She tried to ignore it, telling herself that she was being ridiculous.

The battle between her fingers and her mind went on for what felt like minutes. *Don't*, a voice inside her head blared, but before she could stop herself, she was pressing the camera's home button.

A gasp escaped her lips as the small screen lit up with the face of a girl.

Her brown eyes were hollow and her small face was so devoid of emotion that she could have been a statue. Her long hair flowed down her back, and she wore earrings, little silver balls.

Unable to stop herself, Cassidy clicked the back arrow. In the frame was another girl—similar in age, sitting in a chair, the back-ground dark and empty, her gaze off to the side, as if watching someone. Her white shirt had a curved collar. The kind school uniforms would have.

Cassidy put the camera back, her fingers shaking. Carefully she unplugged her phone and replugged Mel's, trying to remember exactly where it and the camera had been, then rolled the desktop down, inch by slow inch.

Her heart beat so hard it hurt her ears, and a nauseous churning in her gut told her she would soon be sick. She hurried back across the floor, praying she wouldn't trip, to stuff her things into her backpack, trading them for the items she would need: hiking boots, socks, long pants.

There was only one thought in her mind: *Run.*

TWENTY-FIVE

CASSIDY WAS TUGGING on her T-shirt when the floor above her creaked. Carefully, she turned around, her eyes fixed on the stairway. Another gust gently rocked the treehouse. She waited through another eternal moment and then, with no sounds from above, slipped on her socks and pants that were so grubby from fieldwork the fabric crackled, and stepped into her hiking boots.

"Cassidy?" Mel said, appearing halfway on stairs in a pair of pajama pants.

Cassidy froze.

"I thought I heard something," Mel said, rubbing his face and squinting. "What time is it?"

"Early," Cassidy said, swallowing the still-burning bile in her throat.

"What's wrong?" he asked, continuing down the steps.

He looked so genuinely puzzled that she had a moment of doubt. And she so wanted to give in to that doubt. How could this man, this kind, thoughtful man, who seemed to know what she needed before she even knew it herself, who had rescued her from loneliness, from herself, not be real?

Cassidy tried to speak but nothing came. It was like the words were tied to an anchor.

He noticed her outfit, then, and his compassionate look changed. "Cassidy. What's going on?"

Cassidy forced her mind to work. *Think.* "My flight," she stammered. "I have to get there early, and I didn't want to wake you."

Mel seemed to think on this for a moment.

Cassidy swallowed. Should she run for the door? Or could she talk her way out of this?

Mel tilted his head to peer at her. "Your flight isn't until ten, right?"

Her stomach lurched. How did he know the time of her departure? She hadn't given him the details.

Mel's face hardened. In a flash, his gaze traveled to the desk and back to her. "What have you been doing?" he asked, all kindness in his voice gone.

"Me?" she said, her voice a pathetic squeak. "Nothing. I woke up and didn't feel so good, so I thought I'd just walk back to town, and meet my ride."

"No," Mel said. "Try again."

Cassidy resisted the urge to look in the direction of the desk, but it was like Mel could sense its pull on her anyway. A mounting sense of panic took hold as she tried to think her way out of this.

Mel sighed. "I knew it was too risky to bring you here." He ran a hand through his hair. "But I just . . . wanted to feel normal," he said. "You're so . . . good, and sweet, and I haven't had that in a long time, you know?"

Cassidy staggered backwards, but her foot snagged on a pack strap, and she went down hard on her butt.

"I never meant for this to happen. It's not like . . . " He sighed heavily. "But I'm locked in, now. There's no way out." He gazed down at her with a menacing sneer. "I'm afraid there won't be for you, either."

Icy tentacles wrapped around her lungs and squeezed.

"You killed Reeve, didn't you?" Cassidy said from the floor. Could she make a break for it? If she left her pack, she could outrun him. But what about her passport, money? How would she get out of the country?

"If only you'd just kept your nose out of it," Mel said, his eyes flashing with anger.

"He found out about what you do, and you killed him."

"He thought he was so clever," Mel said through gritted teeth. "But nobody steals from me."

"Steal? You mean Jade?" she asked, the connections coming together too fast in her mind.

"It's not like I didn't know where that boat would end up."

"But she got away, didn't she?" If she moved slowly enough, would he notice her inching towards the door?

Mel's gritted teeth flashed in the darkness.

"Wait, you were in my room! In San Juan." Cassidy remembered her hotel room and her pile of clothes that had not been the way she had left them.

Mel walked to the kitchen counter and grabbed his keys.

Cassidy eyed the door but it was too far away. "What were you looking for?"

"His phone," he said.

Cassidy realized that she still had it, in the bottom of her pack, the battery in a separate pouch. "If I give it to you, will you let me go?"

Mel stood at the edge of the counter, backlit by the pale green glow from the kitchen. "I almost had a lucky break when he attacked Juno."

Cassidy inhaled sharply. Juno was the taxi driver!

"But he got off with a fine," Mel continued, removing a small case from a cupboard above the refrigerator. He slid the case and keys into his pocket. "If only Reeve would have killed him, then my troubles would have ended there."

"How can you even talk like that?" Cassidy said, unable to keep her disgust from her quavering voice. "These are human beings. The girls, they're just children. How could you do this to them?"

In one swoop, he reached down and yanked her to her feet. "That's enough of that. It's time to go."

"No!" Cassidy sobbed, unable to stop the terror from taking hold in her heart.

Mel looked her in the eyes, and his gaze softened. "I wish I didn't have to do this." He scooped up her pack and thrust it at her.

Quivering with cold fear, Cassidy slung a pack strap over her shoulder. That's when she remembered the multi-tool attached to her hip belt. Was it still there? Cassidy's fingers traced the edge to the nylon case. She wiggled one finger beneath the Velcro flap, finding the hard metal edge in place.

"No stalling!" Mel barked, and tugged on her arm.

Her breath ragged, she stumbled forward, managing to slide the other shoulder strap on. With fingers shaking in fear, she carefully pulled open the flap.

Mel opened the door, pulling her along as he did, and turned just as she plucked the tool from her belt and folded it into her closed fist.

Outside, the cacophony of the insect sounds exploded in her ears. Grateful for the cover of darkness, Cassidy stumbled behind Mel onto the stairway, her right hand trying to access the knife. But the knife was tucked inside a row of other tools—a screwdriver head, a small pair of scissors, a bottle opener. Removing any of them was a tricky task with two hands, but she had to do it with just one.

They were descending the stairs step by step, the movements jerky from Mel pulling on her arm.

"I can do it!" she yelled when he pulled too hard, forcing her to crash into the railing. But he didn't stop, and they continued down. Desperate, she brought her hands together, low and shielded from him until he turned around. *I'll only have one shot at this.* She opened the tool and felt for the correct groove in the knife.

Was the knife the first tool, or in the middle? She felt the edge of the first tool—yes! It was the knife. She pinched its groove with her thumbnail and pulled.

Just at that moment they reached the halfway, where the stairs reversed direction. Mel's sudden shift in movement yanked her arm forcefully, pulling her hands apart. The knife, open and locked in place, flew through the air, landing on the platform with a clatter.

Mel turned sharply and noticed the knife. Panic flooded her. She swung her backpack off one shoulder and into Mel. With a grunt of surprise, he let go of her arm.

Cassidy dove for the knife, her fingers scrabbling over the wood in the dark. Had it fallen through one of the stairs? Instantly, Mel was on her, his body weight crushing her, his hands searching the platform for the knife too. She writhed and bucked and fought with all her strength. Then the knife was in her hands. She jabbed it back in his direction, slicing the air.

Breathing heavily, Mel grabbed at the knife—easing the pressure on her left side just enough to give her some freedom. Gripping the knife in her right hand, she rolled hard and swung. The knife hit something firm and Mel cried out. Cassidy scrambled backwards, unable to breathe. What had she hit? Mel's side? His neck?

She didn't wait to find out. She lurched for the railing and swung her legs over. How far was she from the ground? Ten feet? six? Before she could push off, Mel grabbed her.

She fought, kicking and slashing at the air with the knife, but he dragged her over the railing and slammed her wrist into the platform. Pain exploded in the back of her hand. She struggled to get it free, but he slammed it down again.

This time, something popped. She cried out as white-hot agony shot through her hand. Her world narrowed to just this pain. That and the certainty that she had lost the knife.

Breathing fast, Mel climbed on top of her, pinning her arms to her sides with his knees. A fresh bolt of pain shot through her hand as he squeezed it into her thigh.

"I was going to wait," he said, struggling to remove something from his pocket. "But I can see that we're going to need to do this now."

Cassidy began to cry silent tears. She had fought her hardest, and lost. Mel had her in his clutches, and whatever happened next, she would be powerless to stop it.

Her tears trailed past her temples and into her hair. This couldn't be happening. How could she have let this happen? Clever Cassidy and her curiosity. Why had she let herself come to this place? Why hadn't she kept her room at Hotel Pacifica?

Because she couldn't bear the thought of being alone among all those happy people, the college kids with their carefree life and full social calendars, kids with their whole happy lives ahead of them.

But at least she would have been safe.

Right now, she was more alone than she had ever felt.

Cassidy felt limp, resigned. A drop of blood hit her chest—from his shoulder. So she had stabbed him there, she thought, but how deep was the wound? Could she overpower him somehow? Get the knife back?

On the platform next to her shoulder, he unzipped something, then he lifted what looked like a needle.

"What are you doing?" she whimpered, recoiling. She tried to buck him off but she could barely breathe with his weight on her chest.

"I'm doing you a favor," he said, his voice calm. "It's the best way to go, trust me."

"Wait, no!" she cried, her whole body electrified with the purpose of stopping him. He shifted his position down her torso, then bent over her arm. She felt the brush of his fingers on the inside of her elbow, feeling for what, she didn't understand.

"Please!" she cried out, arching her body with every last shred of strength.

He uncapped the syringe with his teeth, then plunged the hot needle under her skin.

She whimpered with confusion and fear. What had he...?

A rush of euphoria flowed through her so fast she gasped. Sweetness, pure and bright, slammed into her, carrying her off like a magic carpet. She was floating, soaring, a feeling of peace and joy and light filling every corner of her being. Higher and higher she glided. Everything was beautiful, and perfect, and would go on being perfect, forever. She flew over the trees and the ocean, watching surfers ride waves from above, and a pod of dolphins swimming, and beyond, to an island where tropical flowers swayed in a sea breeze with a magical-sounding *shhuussssh*.

Cassidy wondered if she was breathing, or if maybe she didn't need to breathe anymore, ever again. Maybe she had become part of the air. Why had she never found this before? All of her sadness vanished. All of her worry, frustration, fear: gone. This was marvelous!

A hand stroked her face, putting her further at ease. She remembered her father stroking her forehead at night to help her fall asleep, or to soothe her when she was sick. The sensation of joy sweetened even further, as if her father's warmth was inside her, lifting her higher into the clouds. She had the sensation of being carried, the arms holding her strong and sure. Was her father carrying her? It didn't matter where he took her. What mattered was this feeling of warmth and euphoria.

Cassidy wanted the bright, lovely happiness to go on forever and ever, so she would never have to feel the sadness and pain again.

But the sweetness began to fade. She searched for someone to blame. Who was taking this wonderful feeling away from her? Instantly she wanted more of it so she could go back into the clouds and fly, so her heart could be filled with peace.

The sensation faded further. A gray fog enveloped her. She fought the sense of annoyance. What was happening? There was movement. She was in the back of a car. A strange, frustrated edge pushed the edge of her sanity. Where was she going? In her mind, she saw plane on a tarmac, but she couldn't place where it was or why it had appeared.

To her alarm, her body became heavy, and a chill prickled her skin. Her limbs felt like giant tree branches; she was a tree growing through Mel's house. She started to cry but her hands couldn't wipe the tears away. Why couldn't she move? A shiver rattled through her. Sleep tugged at her, drew her down. Cassidy was more tired than she had ever felt.

Cassidy closed her eyes, but Pete was there, his face pinched in fury. It hurt to see him so angry. What had she done to upset him?

From far away, she heard shouting. Was Pete yelling at her? She tried to say that she was sorry. For whatever she had done. For not being there when he died, for letting him down, for forgetting what he smelled like, and the musical sound of his laughter, and all the other things that would soon follow until there was nothing left.

The shouting came closer, bringing the smell of engines and light, so much light. She wanted the too-bright light to go out so she could sleep. So she could go to Pete and tell him she was sorry, and feel his arms embrace her again. So he could forgive her, and all of this could end.

TWENTY-SIX

CASSIDY WOKE SLOWLY to a sense of malaise so powerful she wanted to cry, but everything felt heavy, like she was deep under-water with little hope of reaching the surface.

With a start, she opened her eyes, her heartbeat reverberating against her ribs. Where was she? Where was Mel?

Someone must have removed her contacts from her eyes, because everything was blurry. But it was easy to know where she was because of the bed and the room and the beeping.

She was alone, in a hospital room. Heavy blankets lay across her body, and as she stirred in the bed, the IV in her arm shifted too.

Outside her door, men and women shuffled past—blips of fuzzy color, phrases in Spanish, the muted tone of an intercom.

How had she ended up here? The last thing she remembered was the sensation of floating—the glorious, precious feeling of utter peace and beauty—more joy than she had ever experienced, and probably never would again.

A wave of despair washed over her. How had this happened to her?

She remembered Pete's fury. Someone yelling at her. Pete? Someone had carried her. Had it been Mel, or Pete?

The logical side of her brain laid out the facts: Mel had injected her with some kind of drug, delivering a powerful high.

The sensation of anger and heaviness—that was her dying.

A man entered the room, and though he was blurry, she immediately knew his face.

Bruce.

"Cassidy, you're awake," he said, striding to the side of her bed.

He quickly placed the cup of coffee he had been carrying on the side table. "Jeez, you gave us a scare."

Cassidy looked away, tears pricking at the edges of her eyes.

"I thought you were on a plane to LA," he said.

She swallowed her tears. "I had to get my things, remember?"

"Right," he said, his voice tense.

"Any chance you know where my glasses are?" she asked, her voice thin.

"Got 'em," he said, striding to the closet and removing a bag.

He returned to her side and slid her glasses onto her face. The world came into crisp focus, bringing on a powerful sense of relief. But Bruce's brown eyes were so full of kindness, his posture hunched and tense, that it made her start to cry all over again.

"What happened, Bruce? How did I end up here?" she asked.

Bruce sat down and cleared his throat. "You had overdosed. Our team got there . . . " He paused to scrape his stubbled chin.

"Wait," she said. "*Our* team?"

He clasped his hands and braced his elbows on his knees. "Yeah. Maybe we should start over." He sighed. "I'm a federal agent for a special unit of the Justice Department. Homeland Security, actually. Costa Rica's OIJ is involved too. We formed a special task force to fight human trafficking in this region."

Her foggy brain processed this in bits and pieces. Flashes of memory hit her like shrapnel—the hotel manager he'd paid in Playas del Coco, the way he'd so eagerly chased their pursuers in San Juan and how he'd jumped her aboard the *Trinity*. The gun.

"Oh my God," she finally said, blinking at the ceiling. "Mel, he and that guy Juno, they...I think they killed Reeve."

"Last night we finally had enough evidence to bring Mel down."

Cassidy gasped as the memories came flooding back. The treehouse, the peaceful dinner on the porch, the feeling that she was safe, cared for, Mel's gentle touch, and his tenderness. A sob choked in her throat, and despair came down on her again like a flood.

How could I have put my trust in such a monster?

"Hey, hey," Bruce said, moving closer, touching her shoulder. "He's going to get locked away for a long time, okay?"

Cassidy nodded, not because she cared about Mel being punished, but because it was easier than explaining the feelings swirling around in her head: her shame at being deceived, the emptiness now that she was once again alone, and her frustration that she had been unable to save herself.

Bruce ran a hand through his hair. "I had no idea you were there."

"I didn't...plan to be," Cassidy said, and closed her eyes. A dull but persistent headache was making it hard to think. She explained about the hotel room and getting lost and later, what she had seen on Mel's camera, and how the image of Juno's face on his phone screen had connected all the dots.

"Please don't think I'm the kind of person who would be connected to someone like that," she said.

"I don't," Bruce said, his eyes kind. "He was a master at deception, if that makes you feel any better. He's fooled a lot of people—including me."

Cassidy released a heavy sigh. "Did I . . . die?"

Bruce frowned, his eyes darkening. "Our kits have Naloxone. Otherwise, you would have."

"I remember...feeling heavy, like I was made of lead, and not being able to breathe," Cassidy said, gazing about the room, taking it all in: the TV on the wall opposite her, and the tubes and bags of fluids hanging from their poles, and the monitor with a sensor attached to her arm. As if noticing it had conjured it to life, it automatically squeezed her arm, then released.

Bruce frowned at the numbers that popped up on the monitor. "Your blood pressure is still low."

"Can I still make my flight?" Cassidy asked.

Bruce gave her a sharp look. "You've already missed it, Cassidy. You've been out for almost ten hours."

Cassidy fought her annoyance. "I need to get home, Bruce."

He shook his head. "You're not going anywhere for at least a few days."

"A few days?" Cassidy cried, sitting upright.

Bruce put up his hands. "You can't just jump up and walk out of here, not yet." He nodded at the machinery. "It's not safe. Your body is still metabolizing the drug. You might need more medicine. Your hand needs a cast."

At this, she looked at her left hand, which was wrapped in a giant bandage. She could see the purple tips of her middle and ring finger poking out. "Is it broken?" she asked.

Bruce nodded. "Two metatarsals. At least you don't need surgery. You'll have to lay off typing for a while, though." He smiled at his joke, but it faded again when he saw her reaction. She appreciated his attempts to make her feel better, but it was like she was dead inside.

"My ring!" she gasped in a panic, wiggling her fingers inside her cast.

Bruce grimaced. "They had to cut it off."

A new wave of despair crashed over her. Pete's ring, the one he had created for her to wear for the rest of her life. Gone.

"It was that or lose your finger." He sighed. "I'm sorry."

Cassidy couldn't look at him. Tears blurred her vision and she wiped them away with her good hand.

"Thank you for saving my life," she said with difficulty.

"You saved mine. Consider the score even." His calm, steady voice downshifted her tension. "I'm going to let you rest," he said, and rose.

Cassidy knew that she was pushing him away, but it couldn't be helped. "When it was happening," she said. "I saw Pete. He was angry with me for something. He was shouting."

Bruce gave her a compassionate smile. "That was me, Cass," he said. "You don't remember what I was yelling?"

Cassidy searched her memories for the answer, but came up empty.

"I was yelling at you to fight, to not give up."

The memory returned sharp and loud. *Come back to me, Cassidy,* Bruce had shouted. *You can do this!*

Those words had given her the strength to push through the heavy darkness to the light.

"Will I be okay?" she asked him, fighting back more tears. "I mean, am I . . . " She knew what addicts went through to get clean. Was she going to have to walk that horrible road?

"You'll go through withdrawals, which are going to suck, but then you'll be okay." He paused. "You're not an addict."

Cassidy lay back into the pillows. The news came as a relief, but it was only temporary because the malaise was there waiting for her. A craving she knew she'd never be able to satisfy.

"That euphoria, it was . . . incredible." Cassidy looked at Bruce squarely, wanting to share this. So much of Reeve's battle had been secret, hidden. She didn't want any secrets.

"I understand now why people do it and can't stop. It's awful."

"I'm so sorry you had to go through this, Cassidy." He stood and smiled. "But it's going to be okay."

Cassidy turned away and sucked in a breath. Bruce was wrong. This was so far from okay.

. . .

SHE WOKE IN DARKNESS. Her glasses rested on the small table next to her, along with a Styrofoam cup with a straw. Gratefully, she took a long gulp of the ice water and slipped on her glasses.

The sounds from outside the room were infrequent, though an occasional alarm or muted conversation made its way through the cracks. She thought back to everything that Bruce had told her.

Bruce had been working undercover—that she understood. So did that mean that he had used her somehow? When Reeve went missing, it had to have been a problem for him. Had she helped or hindered his investigation?

And had the relaxing night they'd shared under the stars been genuine? She had felt a connection to him then—could she trust it, or was it all a front so that he could keep tabs on her?

That night he had told her about growing up in Hawaii, about his family, about surfing the North Shore. Had those stories been made up as part of his cover? Her foggy brain quickly hit overwhelm.

Would she ever truly understand the events that had led her here?

TWENTY-SEVEN

BY THE TIME the doctors released her from the hospital, Cassidy felt much stronger. Her hand no longer throbbed, her lungs didn't feel raspy, and her brutal headache had faded to almost nothing. She picked through her clothes, selecting the long, cotton skirt she had saved for the flight home, and her only remaining clean shirt, a long-sleeved button-down meant to act as a sun shirt. Pete's ring, sliced by the emergency team, was tucked away in her pack. *I guess I have an answer to Héctor's question now*, she thought with bitterness.

Cassidy signed the paperwork, and listened to the doctor's discharge instructions, then waited for her escort. A middle-aged man arrived, dressed in scrubs, his brown eyes weary. He checked her wristband against his paperwork, and then helped her climb into the wheelchair. The man grabbed her pack, grunting with the weight, and then she was gliding down the glossy corridor.

At the curb, a sleek black SUV was idling. The hot air outside of the air-conditioned hospital baked her mouth dry.

A thick-chested Tico exited the passenger side. "Yo, Cassi-dee," he said in a heavy accent and pointed to his wide chest. "Alonso."

Cassidy frowned. Had the hospital called for this deluxe ride? She had requested a taxi.

Alonso took her things from the medical assistant and placed them in the back of the SUV, then opened the passenger door.

Waiting inside was Bruce.

Alonso reached for her hand, but Cassidy was already on her feet. She stepped away from the wheelchair.

"*Listo?*" Alonso asked.

Cassidy climbed inside the backseat. Alonso closed her door, then slid behind the wheel.

"Alo was there that night," Bruce said.

Cassidy caught his grimace before she looked away. What had Alonso seen that night?

The SUV pulled away from the curb. "Temperature ok-eh?" he asked her, gazing in the rearview mirror.

"Fine, thank you," Cassidy said, then glanced at Bruce.

"I didn't think I was going to see you again," she said. "They aren't coming for you now, are they?"

Bruce smiled. "I'll be leaving the country soon, sure, but until then, I have Alo." He nodded to the driver.

"What will happen to . . . everybody?" she finally managed.

"The Americans will be extradited. The Costa Ricans will be tried here."

"What about the children?" she asked as the images from the camera flashed into her mind.

"We're working on that," he said.

Cassidy looked out the window at the lush green flashing by. "Did you know about Reeve all along?" she asked.

Bruce gave her a pensive glance. "I knew something was going on beyond him just disappearing. There was actually a comment he made about Mel that helped me piece something together, but it wasn't until I followed those goons who chased us that I made sense of it."

"I thought you said that chase didn't lead anywhere? That it got too conspicuous."

Bruce stubbed his chin. "Let's just say I had some help after that, and we found the evidence we needed to bring in Mel." He glanced at her, his eyes pained. "We also found several graves."

Cassidy inhaled a sharp breath. "Reeve's?"

Bruce grimaced. "I believe so. I'll know for sure in a few days."

Cassidy slumped against the window. She had known he was dead all along, but now that it was real, that she had failed—in so many ways—that same heaviness she'd been fighting since waking up returned.

"I'm sorry," Bruce said.

The SUV turned onto a highway and they sped north, the green jungle of tall, lofty canopies flying past in a blur. To the East, the dark volcanic mountains poked out of the olive-brown haze. Though she couldn't see Arenal from this vantage point, it was enough to know it was there.

But would she ever be back to complete her research?

Ten minutes later, they turned off the highway at the Liberia airport. Cassidy gazed at the pale, cracked concrete and travelers rushing in and out of the modern building.

"Will I have to testify?" she asked Bruce.

"I hope not," he said, looking thoughtful. "I'll do what I can to protect you."

Cassidy breathed a sigh of relief. "Thank you."

"You know, if you ever get tired of saving the world from volcanic eruptions, you should think about detective work." Bruce grinned. "You're a natural."

A dry chuckle escaped from her lips.

"Actually," he added, his eyes growing serious. "There's something I wanted to tell you."

A flutter of fear tickled her insides. "Oh," she said.

He gave her a tight nod, and continued, "This chain of human trafficking doesn't stop in Central America. It extends all the way into the States. This particular group of scumbags imports to Los Angeles and San Francisco."

Cassidy squinted at him. "Why are you telling me this?"

"While I was waiting for you to wake up, I looked up Pete's work. I've actually read that story of his on the Hernandez family."

Inside her chest, a steamroller flattened her heart. "And?"

Bruce shrugged. "Just that, well . . . He was fighting the same war that I'm fighting. That we're fighting." He glanced at Alonso, who nodded.

"I wish I could do something to erase all the terrible things that happened to you," he said. "But I wanted you to know that it made a difference. That what you did and what Reeve did, it meant something. And Pete, what he was doing, it helped, too. I think Pete would be proud of you—the risks you took and your bravery."

Cassidy was crying before he finished his sentence. She wanted it to be true, to imagine Pete beaming his biggest smile at her as he folded her into his arms. "Well done, Kinney," he might say.

But all she could remember was his angry posture, his yelling. A spark of anger flared inside her. Wasn't he the one who left? She should be the one yelling at *him*.

Now Reeve was gone, too, and though their relationship had never been strong, losing him brought everything back.

"He didn't die in vain," Bruce was saying.

Alonso pulled up to the curb and parked and slid out of the SUV to grab her things.

"Here," Bruce said, and handed her a white card with a single phone number. "Reach me anytime, okay?"

Cassidy took the card and stuffed in her pocket.

"Goodbye, Cass," he said.

Cassidy gave him one last glance and stepped into the sun.

WHEN SHE EXITED the long tunnel of customs in LAX, three tanned faces were waiting for her.

"Cassideeeeee!" Taylor shrieked. Benita and Libby followed, all crushing her in a tight hug.

Libby grabbed her shoulders and stared into her eyes. "You. Look. Worked."

Cassidy smiled. "Definitely. But it's great to see you guys. How did you know I was here?"

"A little birdie told us," Benita said, crossing her arms.

Bruce, Cassidy thought.

"Who do you think brought you all of your stuff?" Taylor said.

"But I didn't see you guys," Cassidy protested.

"You were still, like, in a coma when we came. The docs made us go in one at a time."

Overcome with contentment to see these women who had become trusted friends, Cassidy just managed to hold in her tears. "I wasn't sure if I would see you guys again."

"Hey," Benita said. "You remember what I said, right? Us surf sisters gotta stick together."

Cassidy grinned.

"So, you got a few hours, right?" she asked.

Cassidy checked her ticket, and her watch. "About three."

"Perfect," Benita said.

Libby grabbed her pack from her back, and Taylor put her arm around Cassidy's shoulders. "You don't have to tell us anything about what happened," she said, leading her to the gritty curb outside.

"We're just glad to see you again, girl," Libby added.

MARISSA AND JILLIAN were waiting at a corner table in a restaurant that Cassidy didn't get the name of. Soon they were ordering drinks, and seemingly within minutes, food arrived—the kind she hadn't eaten for weeks: a green salad with creamy ranch dressing and carrots, peppers, and avocado, a hamburger with a sourdough bun and melted cheddar cheese.

The women filled her in on the rest of their journey home and how they had been so worried about her.

Cassidy kept Bruce's secret mission to herself. Maybe the story would make the news someday, and then they would know. Or maybe Bruce's involvement would remain a secret. Like a superhero's.

He didn't die in vain, Bruce had said. In the back of the SUV at the curb in Liberia, she had assumed he meant Reeve. But could he have been talking about Pete? Cassidy shook her head. No, he had meant Reeve. Pete crashed his motorcycle while driving too fast in San Francisco.

"You aren't drinking your Greyhound," Jillian said, sipping hers. "Is it okay? Want me to get them to use a different vodka? They probably have Ketel One."

Cassidy took a deep breath. "I'm not drinking."

"Aw, come on, you've earned it," Marissa said.

Cassidy shook her head. "Thanks anyways," she added, trying to make her voice sound light. "I've had enough chemicals in my blood for a while."

They laughed it off, so likely missed her adding, "Maybe forever."

BENITA JUMPED down to the curb and gave her one last hug. "We're sisters for life, you know that, right?"

Cassidy so badly wanted to stay with her "sister surfers" and bask in their friendship just a little longer, but it was time to go home.

"I know," Cassidy said, sliding her pack off to unbuckle the ukulele strapped to it. "I think this belongs to you now," she said, offering it.

Benita gave her a wary look.

"Reeve would want you to have it," Cassidy added. "Or your son. Someone to play it. Keep it alive."

"You don't want to try playing it? Maybe you'll learn how someday."

Cassidy shook her head. "You helped me find him," she said, her eyes starting to burn. "I want you to have it."

Benita gave her a long hug and then took the instrument. "I'll see you again," she said. "And in the meantime, if anybody ever messes with you, I got your back, okay?"

Cassidy laughed to cover the start of more tears. "Okay," she said, then hoisted her backpack and waved at her friends.

"Bye!" they all yelled as Cassidy turned and sprinted through the doors.

TWENTY-EIGHT

THREE DAYS after Cassidy had returned home and shared Reeve's fate with Pamela and Rebecca, a story ran in the Ventura paper about Reeve. Cassidy's phone began ringing nonstop. The first time, she answered it without thinking. It was a reporter for the *Los Angeles Times*.

"I'll bet it feels good to be back in the USA after your ordeal."

"Wait," she said, disoriented. "Who is this?"

"Everyone's calling you a hero. What do you think about that?"

Cassidy tried to formulate a reply, but the reporter kept talking.

"Were you there when they dug up Reeve's body?"

"How did you get this number?" Cassidy interrupted, gasping for breath.

"Your mom gave it to me," he replied, then added, not missing a beat, "Did Reeve plan to rescue more sex slaves?"

"My mom is dead," Cassidy hissed and hung up.

Cassidy had not talked about the trip with anyone, but some of her colleagues knew that she had broken her hand while trying to track down her stepbrother. No one knew about what Mel had done to her in the treehouse, and she hoped she would never have to talk about it in the department. Her colleagues and her staff already thought she was fragile because of her breakdown after Pete's death.

Jay, on the other hand, had enough material to last them a lifetime. Reeve's death had brought on terrible feelings associated with Pete's accident, and also the death of her parents, but Jay was careful not to push her too hard.

After the L.A. Times reporter incident, Cassidy double-checked every incoming number and only answered calls from trusted sources. The stories in the weeks following her return from Costa Rica offered a diffuse version of the truth. It was possible that Cassidy was their only link to what happened. Eventually, the phone calls trickled to a stop.

However, she did receive one email from a woman named Sharon Lee of Operation Break the Chain, a rescue organization partnered with Tikvah International.

It was a message she was happy to open.

Dear Dr. Kincaid,

Thank you for your inquiry. Children entering our care in Texas choose a new identity as part of their rehabilitation and healing process. I am happy to say, however, that I believe the young woman in question did arrive safely on November 7. I will place your letter in safekeeping and let her choose to read it, but only if and when she is ready. Most children choose to break all ties to their former life when they enter our program. We encourage this step of independence. I hope you understand. However, I will personally share the news of your stepbrother's passing with her, as this may factor into her healing process.

I offer you my sincerest condolences.

In peace,
Sharon Lee, Director, Operation Break the Chain

CASSIDY HAD MADE a donation in Reeve's name—the maximum amount that Rodney, the shrewd financial advisor her father had hired to oversee her accounts, would permit. It still didn't feel like enough. In a follow-up email, Sharon did agree to keep Cassidy informed of any special needs she could assist with—anonymously, of course. Anything that could help Jade start a new life: tuition or job assistance, or even money to travel someday. Cassidy even went so far as to research what type of bicycle Jade might want, and how she could send it to her. The image of Jade pedaling through some small town with the wind in her hair filled her with hope.

IT TOOK Pamela until early February to organize the service because of the difficulty of reclaiming Reeve's remains. Plus, the holidays had been upon them, and nobody wanted to attend a funeral at Christmas.

Cassidy had survived the season only by diving into her work—and surfing. Whenever a big swell hit the coast, she was there with her thermos of coffee and bagel sandwiches at dawn to paddle out at first light. She had not even bought a Christmas tree or played any holiday music. Too risky.

Reeve's service was held in the small church overlooking the ocean, a place Cassidy had never visited but that Pamela had apparently attended with Reeve and Rebecca when they were children. The pastor had read a soothing passage, punctuated by mourners sniffing into their tissues. Then they had sung a hymn, their collective voices filling the somber space.

Now at the gravesite, under Quinn's umbrella, Cassidy huddled close to her brother. Her high-heeled shoes sunk into the wet grass, forcing her to shift her feet occasionally, which made her nylons rub together and itch her legs even more. The winter day had dawned gray, with the rain starting soon after she and Quinn had shared a quiet breakfast in his cold apartment.

Reeve would have a shiny granite plaque in the church's cemetery, but his ashes would be scattered. Pamela would do most of this, but Cassidy had asked for a portion that she could set adrift with Quinn near his home in San Francisco. Letting a part of Reeve be free to roam the ocean he loved so much was a duty she could not forsake.

When it was her turn, she stepped forward and placed her flowers on Reeve's memorial. Then she let Quinn put his arm around her and lead her back to the car.

Most of the guests at Reeve's Celebration of Life were family members Cassidy had never met. They hugged Pamela, who put on a brave face but broke down several times. Rebecca stood stoically by her side, her face a mask of pain.

THE DAY after the memorial dawned cold and breezy, with overcast skies and veils of fog that moved through the trees like ghosts.

"You sure about this?" Quinn asked as they sipped espresso brewed from his Italian stovetop percolator. The heat coming through the baseboard warmed her toes. Cassidy savored it, because the water temperature hovered in the low fifties. "We could wait until the summer. The water doesn't get much warmer, but at least we might have sunshine."

Cassidy shook her head. Pete's ashes were still packed in their box in Eugene. One dead person in her house was enough.

They drove the short distance to the beach, where ocean breakers thumped onto the sandy shore. Cars lined the parking lot, with a few surfers gearing up in their black wetsuits, waxing their boards, or checking the surf, coffee cup in hand. The waves were messy thanks to a brisk onshore breeze, but a few surfers dotted the lineups.

She and Quinn changed into their neoprene wetsuits—Quinn in a 5/4 borrowed from a friend, and Cassidy in the winter suit she had packed next to her heels and black wool dress, her jewelry case and pajamas.

"You remember how to do this?" she asked Quinn, squinting at him through the tight opening in her hood.

"I guess we'll find out. You remember how to save me if I start to drown?" His gray-blue eyes twinkled.

Cassidy tried to smile, but it felt more like a twitch.

They grabbed their boards from the roof, and she clipped the dry bag containing Reeve's remains around her waist. Then the two of them walked down the steps to the cold sand. None of the surfers at Ocean Beach wore booties or gloves, even in February—a code of toughness. Cassidy felt the need to comply, for Reeve, even though she couldn't explain its importance.

The icy water froze her toes instantly, and the heavy water pushed and pulled at her as she waded in. When a lull came, she hopped on her board and began paddling hard. The dry bag rolled side to side against her lower back as she moved.

Her first duck dive beneath a line of breakers froze her cheeks and forehead. Reeve's dry bag resisted submersion and she almost didn't get under the wave. After Quinn popped up next to her, they stroked and dove under another wave, and another, until she lost count and the effort took over her whole being.

When she finally surfaced to see unbroken, shifting ocean, her entire body shuddered with relief.

"I'll never understand why you think this is fun," Quinn said, panting.

"Sometimes it's not fun," she replied. Her shoulder muscles throbbed with a pleasant ache, and her core was warm from the battle. "It's necessary."

As a marathon runner, Quinn would understand this logic.

They sat on their boards for a moment, catching their breath. Cassidy monitored their position against the incoming waves, making sure they didn't drift too far inside or get caught in a rip.

"Shall we do this and get out of here before we get clobbered?" Quinn said, his wet eyelashes thick and dark against his pale, freckled cheeks.

Cassidy unclipped the dry bag and opened it, her breaths shaky with the strain of balancing while reaching in to remove a plastic bag.

Last spring, she had completed just such an endeavor with some of Pete's ashes on Mt. St. Helens, the special place where she had first studied and where he'd proposed.

And here she was orchestrating yet another burial. A deep ache settled into her bones.

Quinn took the bag from her while Cassidy re-clipped the empty container back onto her waist, her frozen fingers fumbling with the clasp.

"Well, Reeve," Quinn said, eyeing Cassidy. "Here's to a happy afterlife." He handed the bag to Cassidy.

She looked at the gray ashes. "I'm sorry," she said as the ache inside her intensified, stealing her breath. "I never gave you a second chance. And I wasn't there for you."

"Hey," Quinn said. "You're here now, okay? Quit beating yourself up. Reeve wouldn't want that."

Cassidy gazed past him to the blue expanse. "But if I had taken his call, maybe I could have done something."

Quinn shook his head. "You were going through hell when he called. And you were in Eugene. What could you have done?"

A part of her craved this relief, but the deep belief that she had failed Reeve persisted.

"You tried, Cass," Quinn said. "And it almost cost you your life." He gripped her shoulder. "I think it's safe to say you did your best. It's okay to let him go."

Cassidy took a deep breath and tore open the bag. Gritty ash spilled into the ocean, some of it sinking, some of it floating off on the current.

Quinn reached for her hand, and the two of them watched it all disappear.

TWENTY-NINE

CASSIDY WHEELED her suitcase up the cracked walkway to her house. Though gone for only four days in California, it felt longer. Quinn had offered to take some time off and come with her, but getting back to her life was a priority.

When she unlocked her door and stepped inside, the emptiness enveloped her like a cold draft. After removing her shoes, parking her suitcase by the couch, and turning on the heat, she poured herself a glass of water from the kitchen sink. The stove light shone over the empty range, with a welcome home note from her neighbor, a retired schoolteacher whom Cassidy had asked to collect her mail and check on the house. The previous tenants must have spent a lot of money ordering clothes and electronics, because every day her mailbox was stuffed full of catalogues. Though there was a phone number she could call to stop this ridiculous waste of paper, somehow she never took the time to look it up.

Cassidy scooped up the bundle and headed for the recycle bin when the yellow edge of a manila envelope peeked out from the colorful glossies.

The return stamp read Library of Congress in Washington D.C.

She had almost forgotten her request for all of Pete's articles, and here it finally was.

The idea had come to her weeks ago. She had been in her office, looking for a receipt so she could submit it for reimbursement when she came across a stub for a baseball game that she, Pete, and Reeve had attended during his visit to Eugene. Pete and Reeve were talking about one of Pete's stories in between bites of hot dog and sips of beer.

Cassidy remembered Reeve asking: "That story you did about the Hernandez family. How did you know all that stuff?"

Now, standing in her kitchen, with the fat envelope in her hands, the memory flooded into her mind in sharp detail: Pete had worked on that story nonstop for weeks, staying up late, fielding calls from his editor at all hours of the day and night. He had piles of notes—hand scribbled, scraps of pages he had printed, lime-green sticky notes affixed to it all like giant confetti. Pete had cracked big stories before, so this hadn't struck her as particularly odd.

But after the story was published, he started getting mail from readers. The *New Yorker* called, and soon he had his dream job writing for them.

He didn't die in vain. Cassidy had thought Bruce was talking about Reeve. But after the memory of Pete's story surfaced, she wasn't so sure.

She stared at the fat manilla envelope with a sense of purpose but with no tangible goal. What did she expect to find in his words?

Cassidy caressed its yellow surface. The idea of revisiting what had been in Pete's heart and mind, looking for something she could barely sense, let alone understand, pulled at her like an intoxicating puzzle.

The Hernandez family is notoriously ruthless.

Was Bruce suggesting there was a connection between Pete's work and his death?

Cassidy pulled the blanket from the easy chair and draped it around her, and then she sat down on the couch with Pete's stories.

The big window looking over her neglected lawn reflected her slumped posture, and the braid draped over her shoulder, loose about her face.

Cassidy smoothed back the wispy hairs at her forehead and tried to banish the vision of Mel and Pete engaged in a motorcycle chase on a foggy autumn night. Even though she knew this was impossible, the image had been a frequent visitor in her nightmares. Pete died because he was driving too fast on an unfamiliar curve of road. Hadn't he?

Cassidy put the envelope aside and walked to her desk. From inside her filing cabinet, she pulled out the file marked Costa Rica. After opening the file on her desk, she sifted through the receipts and notes she had made while hunting down supplies in San José. There was even a brochure from the Hot Springs Resort near Arenal.

Bruce's card was underneath all of this, a simple phone number. She pulled it out, its crisp corners sharp against her fingertips.

If she was going to walk this road, she couldn't do it alone.

Cassidy flipped Bruce's card over and over, thinking about the way he'd looked at her in the SUV in Liberia.

Like he knew a secret.

Bruce answered on the second ring. "Nice to hear from you, Cassidy," he said, his voice so clear he might have been in her living room.

An emotion she didn't understand rose up inside her. "How did you know it was me?" she asked.

"It's my job to know a lot of things. How are you?" he asked in a tentative voice, as if the question caused him suffering.

Cassidy's fingers tightened around the phone. "I'm okay." She tried to sound brave. No way would she tell him about the nightmares, her daily struggle to feel normal. There were days when she felt productive and could work for long stretches. And then there were the bad days when the veil of hopelessness threatened to suffocate her.

"If there's anything I can do for you—" Bruce began.

"I have all of Pete's stories from the Library of Congress," she said. "Some I remember him writing, some I don't." A wave of guilt washed over her. If she hadn't been so self-absorbed, worrying about publishing and the postdoc and her job search, would she have noticed something?

"I keep thinking about something you said in Costa Rica," she continued, her stomach hard and achy—a pain she apparently caused by not taking enough deep breaths. "There's something you said that keeps replaying in my mind about Pete and the kind of stories he writes."

"What exactly did I say?" Bruce asked in a serious tone.

"You said 'he didn't die in vain.' You were talking about Pete, weren't you?"

There was a long silence, and Cassidy wondered if she had lost the connection.

"All I know is that Pete was digging into some pretty serious stuff," he said, followed by a long, slow exhale.

"So you don't think...Pete's death wasn't an accident?"

Bruce sighed heavily. "Maybe it's best if I don't tell you what I think."

Cassidy's stomach twisted into a hard knot. "Bruce," she managed before a wave of grief wrapped its cold fingers around her heart.

"Let me ask you this," he said. "Did he ever seem afraid?"

Cassidy slumped into her chair. "What do you mean?"

"Did he check the locks on the doors, or did he act hyperaware of what cars were parked on the street? Was he jumpy? Anything like that?"

"No, but when Pete was onto a story, it was like the rest of the world fell away," Cassidy said, rubbing her temple with her free hand. "He loved the thrill that went with the job, you know?"

Bruce sighed. "That's not exactly healthy when dealing with the kind of people he was trying to expose."

"If he was murdered...my God." The knots in her stomach tightened, sending a chill down her spine.

"I don't know that, Cassidy. Like I said, it's just a hunch."

Her hackles jumped to life. "So you're telling me to forget it?"

"Would you do it if I asked?" he replied, his voice tight.

Cassidy waited, trying to tamp down her frustration. Did he suspect Pete's death to be connected to his work or not? Or could his oscillating be attributed to something else—maybe he didn't trust her?

"It just might be better if you left it alone," he added.

So that was it—he didn't want her stirring up trouble.

"I mean, say you get the police to open the case, and miraculously, they agree, and they even find evidence of foul play. What then?"

Her lower back cramped and she had to force a series of breaths into her lungs. "Then they go to jail," she answered, her voice hard.

Bruce sighed. "Okay, let's say justice is served and they do. Then what?"

Cassidy frowned. "What do you mean?"

"I mean, sure, some bad guys get wiped out, and that's awesome. But how will you feel?"

Cassidy didn't understand. Wouldn't she feel great? Victorious?

"It's a long road. A dangerous road. Are you up for the journey? And when it's over, will the effort have brought you what you're looking for?"

"I...don't know," she admitted. "But Bruce, if someone did this to him—" She sucked in a sob. "—I can't just do nothing."

Cassidy thumbed through Pete's notebook, the one he was using at the time of his death. So far she hadn't been able to make sense of his scribbles, sketches, and dates. But what if they, combined with his stories, could shed light on what happened that night?

"Okay," Bruce said, sounding defeated. "What do you want to do?"

"You said if I ever needed anything..." she began.

"Cassidy," he said in a tight voice. "First of all, Pete's death isn't a federal case, which means I have no jurisdiction. And secondly, we have no evidence of foul play."

His use of the plural pronoun didn't escape her. "I'm not expecting you to make a formal inquiry, just...I don't know...steer me in the right direction."

Bruce uttered a long sigh. "All right," he said. "But only because I want to make sure you're not being reckless, okay? If at any time I think you're in danger, we're turning it off."

"Okay," she said, relief flooded her.

"I mean it, Cassidy," he said sternly. "We're entering dangerous territory. I need you to promise that you'll listen to me."

"I promise," she said, at the same time doubting she could keep such a pledge. Especially if she found answers.

"Good," he said. "Okay, here's where we need to start."

WILL CASSIDY BE able to stay out of trouble in her search for the truth, especially when she's pulled into another dangerous missing persons search?

Find out in the next installment of the Cassidy Kincaid mystery series, Finding Izzy Ford.

A missing student. A dark trail of clues. Will Cassidy dig up the real truth in time?

DR. CASSIDY KINCAID survived extreme emotional pressure only to come out stronger. And while teaching the university's summer geology camp has helped distract her from her fiancé's mysterious death, she's eager to return to her ground-breaking volcanic research. But her work studying a critical eruption could go up in smoke when a troubled student disappears on her way back to campus...

Retracing the reckless student's steps, Cassidy can't help but see a foolish young version of herself in the missing girl. So she's terrified of what she finds along a twisted trail of X-rated scandals, biker gangs, and San Francisco's seedy underground. But what she never expected to uncover—was a clue to her own tragic past.

Can Cassidy save the coed and her lifelong ambitions before both vanish without a trace?

Buy Finding Izzy Ford to dig in to this suspenseful mystery today!

KEEP READING FOR A SNEAK PEEK:

Chapter One

Wallowa Lake, Oregon

IF ONLY THE scandal hadn't broken until after field camp ended. Cassidy could have gone back to being anonymous and it wouldn't have hit her so hard.

It started in the bar, of course. After the geology students had packed up all the gear, cleaned up the Boy Scout property serving as their base camp, the entire group walked the gravel road to the lake-side resort for a celebration. Cassidy hung back so she could have the twenty-minute walk to herself. Though she had no intention of hanging out with the students that night while they blew off three weeks of steam, they'd razz her if she didn't at least share one beer.

After three weeks of managing twenty-nine geology majors—camping with them, preparing meals with them, chasing them all over the landscape, reprimanding them for pot smoking or staying up too late, she was ready to reclaim her solitary life. Tomorrow, she and the students would part ways: the students back to Eugene, and Cassidy continuing on to the University of Washington and her new career as a professor of geology.

The late-July blackberry vines lining the gravel road hung heavy with fat berries. Sweetness exploded on her tongue as she popped one into her mouth. But it also triggered memories of Pete and the lazy summer days they'd spent together the summer before he was killed.

She entered the bar, easily identifying her group of students in their trademark t-shirts, shorts, and flip flops, though Martin, one of her graduate students, wore his trademark Madras short sleeve button-down and high-tech running shoes. The students stood clustered together at the end of the bar, their volume overpowering the small space.

As Cassidy crossed the room, a handful of them leaned in to look at something Cody, a bright but lazy student, was showing them on his phone.

"Whoa, seriously?" one of them said as Cassidy leaned against the bar to get the bartender's attention.

Another student, Izzy, her blonde hair tied back in a messy knot, pulled the phone to her face. "Who knew she was such a badass," she said.

"Who's a badass?" Cassidy said, feigning interest. As soon as she had her beer, she would slip away to one of the picnic tables outside. Then, before things got rowdy, she would return to the camp. Martin and her other graduate Bridget would to keep an eye on things.

"You are," Izzy said, flashing the phone in Cassidy's face.

Cassidy blinked. On Cody's phone was a picture of Mel's face.

In an effort to maintain her composure, Cassidy speed-read the passage.

The man, David "Mel" Tomlinson, an accomplice to three members of a Colombian family who lured young women as young as 13 years old to Costa Rica with the promise of good jobs, only to put them to work as prostitutes. All remain in custody as investigators attempt to unravel the complex case. Tomlinson and the three members of the Vasquez family have been charged with 50 counts of human rights violations and if convicted, will serve several life sentences.

Heat flashed over her skin as the fear of that moment in Mel's treehouse came flooding back. Meanwhile, her students stared at her like she was some kind of alien that had dropped out of the sky. Cassidy's blood thumped past her ears as she scanned down to a side-by-side picture of herself and Reeve:

. . . two American victims were involved. Reeve Bennington, a California surf guide was killed while trying to smuggle one of the victims through Nicaragua, and Cassidy Kincaid, a geology student at the University of Oregon, survived an attack by Tomlinson who attempted to cover up his involvement in Bennington's murder.

Kincaid was unable to be reached for this story, but a close family member revealed that Kincaid was in Costa Rica to search for her missing stepbrother, then became tangled in Tomlinson's web. Without Kincaid's help, it's unlikely the truth about Bennington would have surfaced. "He would have remained just another missing person in paradise," ICE special agent Rick Terrel said.

Seeing her face next to Reeve's made her feel hollow. Then came the guilt. Would they have buried her in that unmarked, desert grave next to him? Or dumped her body in the streets of Tamarindo to be labeled as just another overdose? A shiver ran down her spine at the memory of Mel's urgent kisses. Her stomach turned sour.

"So what's the story, Doctor Kincaid?" Cody asked, his sharp expression intensifying. His gray t-shirt displayed a giant pig with the words "Rub My Rump, Then You Can Pull My Pork" floating above it.

Cassidy handed the phone back. "I never intended. . . " she stammered, wishing a breeze off the lake would whoosh in and cool her sweaty forehead.

The bartender, a man with a thick, graying beard and a pencil tucked behind his left ear set down her beer. The sound took her back to Mel serving her Flor on the rocks with that charismatic smile. Cassidy gripped the back of the stool. For weeks she had managed not to think about that terrible night, and now, here it all was, waiting to ambush her.

Alice, Izzy's faithful sidekick, adjusted her thick black glasses. "It's true?" she asked, her big, brown eyes wide.

Cassidy adjusted the strap of her bag against her shoulder. "Yeah," she said finally. "It's true."

"So did you bond with your captor, Dr. Kincaid?" Izzy said, raising her eyebrow.

Cassidy flinched. "No," she managed, as a nauseous tickle crept up her throat.

"How did you escape?" Alice asked. Alice was the quiet kid that never missed an assignment, scored near-perfect on every test. During field camp, she had risen as a kind of star, other students seeking her out for mapping help during the day. Help that Cassidy secretly knew Izzy relied on.

"Did you press charges?" someone else asked. "I certainly would." She recognized William's steady voice.

"Sorry, this . . . is a surprise," Cassidy said, telling herself that everything would be okay if she could just escape to a table outside to sit by herself. *This isn't real*, she reminded herself—her grief counselor Jay's words. *It's over, it's all in the past.* She should probably abandon her beer and go for a run instead, but she had already downed half of it.

"C'mon," Cody groaned. "We haven't read a newsfeed in eight

days and we find out our professor broke up a sex trafficking ring singlehanded? Throw us a bone here."

Cassidy attempted a weak smile, but it only shook loose a sense of failure and sadness. To her horror, she felt her throat thickening with tears.

"Lay off," Izzy said, shooting Cody a loaded look. "I mean, her brother died."

Cassidy resisted the urge to correct Izzy—Reeve wasn't her brother by blood, but his sacrifice to save Jade had made that detail unimportant.

Meanwhile, the others seemed to draw back, as if a spell had been broken.

Cassidy squared her shoulders to the group. Most looked disappointed—Cody even looked suspicious, like he wasn't letting this go so easily. "Thanks for understanding," she said, and carried her beer outside.

Beyond the trees edging the lake, paddleboats and kayaks dotted the shining water, and the sound of outboard motors zooming to and from the dock occasionally filled the air. At the shore below the patio, a lone fisherman stood in his waders casting his line at the creek's inlet.

She settled at a table on the corner of the deck and opened her laptop. The story wasn't hard to find, and as she read it, slowly this time, her body clenched tighter and tighter until she felt like a coiled spring.

...Tomlinson and the three members of the Vasquez family have been charged with 50 counts of human rights violations and if convicted, will serve a minimum of 30 years and as long as several life sentences.

Tomlinson — who coordinated the sex acts using photographs and a website — is facing trial this week. He culled the victims, deciding which would stay in Tamarindo and which would be moved through Mexico to the United States, where they were put to work in massage parlors.

Federal officials agree that the trafficking of human beings as sex slaves is far more prevalent than is popularly understood. While saying it is difficult to pinpoint the scope of the industry, given its shadowy nature, Immigration and Customs Enforcement (ICE) officials estimated that it likely generates more than $9.5 billion a year.

Last year alone, the FBI opened more than 225 human trafficking investigations in the United States. In a coordinated nationwide sweep in December, federal, state and local authorities made more than 640 arrests and rescued 47 children in just three days.

"These young women were either sold or enticed into working as a way to help their families, only to arrive in America and discover that what awaited was a nightmare," said FBI special agent Thomas Kamea.

The 50-count indictment, unsealed Thursday, represents the largest sex trafficking case prosecuted in Southern California by the federal government in at least a decade, the U.S. attorney's office said.

This case is unique because two American victims were involved. Reeve Bennington, a California surf guide was killed while trying to smuggle one of the victims through Nicaragua, and Cassidy Kincaid, a geology student at the University of Oregon, survived an attack by Tomlinson who attempted to cover up his involvement in Bennington's murder.

Kincaid was unable to be reached for this story, but a close family member revealed that Kincaid was in Costa Rica to search for her missing stepbrother, then became tangled in Tomlinson's web. Without Kincaid's help, it's unlikely the truth about Bennington would have surfaced.

So, Mel was going to jail. Cassidy tried to examine her feelings on this but the memory of his brutal hands groping her arm for a vein shoved into her mind instead. She felt the ghost of a prick in her arm followed by the sudden rush of euphoria, as if her brain was a guitar and someone had just strummed the most perfect chord, the sound vibrating the most intense pleasure through her every nerve. She had floated away on this cloud, all her worries left behind. The sensation quickly changed, however, and as the high faded, her body craved that violent sweetness again, her mind desperate for another hit, even while it began to shut down. As the overdose took hold, her body turned limp, her skin burned, but she had been powerless to fight it.

And then Bruce had come.

Her stomach quivered with that same strange feeling. Though she had begged him to help her look into the circumstances of Pete's death, once they started, the journey had overwhelmed her. Her grief counselor, Jay, had urged her to re-evaluate. To push on was to risk the fragile progress she had made.

But now that Mel was headed to jail, maybe things could be different. Maybe she could put the nightmares behind her. Maybe now that she had her new career to look forward to, she would have the energy required for such a pursuit.

Maybe now she was strong enough to start again.

Bruce promised to help her when she was ready.

Cassidy gazed at the serene lake and coaxed a long breath of the sweet summer air into her lungs.

She *was* ready.

It was time to finally get to the bottom of Pete's death.

Keep reading HERE.

FREEBIE ALERT!

READ A SHORT STORY FEATURING FBI AGENT BRUCE KEOLANI BEFORE HE WENT UNDERCOVER FOR FREE!

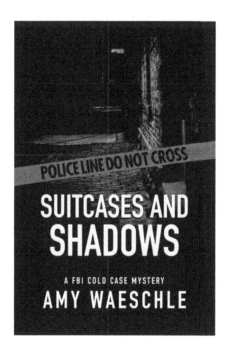

A cold case. A troubled family. The missing clue.

Every cop has a case they can't let go of. The Nash case is rookie

FBI agent Thomas Kamea's. Now that he's a federal agent, maybe the use of their resources plus the advances in technology will help him finally bring the murderer to justice.

Maybe then Cedric Nash's lifeless eyes will stop haunting his nightmares.

But little does Thomas know that the Nash case is a hornet's nest, and he's just kicked it wide open. Will Thomas be able to stay one step ahead of the crafty killer and bring this case to justice? Or will the killer succeed at staying hidden forever?

If you like the rich characters of Kendra Elliot and the suspense and noir of Jeffery Deaver, you'll love this FBI cold case short story.

Get this twisty cold case mystery for free by joining my author community today!

Deadly Secrets - compendium of 13 writers

ALSO BY AMY WAESCHLE

Meg Dawson series

Cassidy Kincaid Series: *- mystery series*

Rescuing Reeve

Finding Izzy Ford

Exposing Ethan

Cassidy's Crusade

The Night Agent

Prequels

Meet Me on the Mountain

(Cassidy & Pete's tragic love story)

Standalone Novels:

self published

Going Over the Falls *- first published*

Feeding the Fire

Memoir:

Chasing Waves, a Surfer's Tale of Obsessive Wandering *2008 or 9*

Short Stories:

Suitcases and Shadows - available in audio!

Swimming Lessons

The Call of the Canyon Wren

Father of the Bride

Daring Rescues - young adult (4th graders)
4 books

Her Final Goodbye - her favorite

ACKNOWLEDGMENTS

I'm grateful to my family for their unwavering support. To my husband who brings me coffee every morning, listens to me work out plot problems while we mountain bike our local trails, and is a superdad to our daughters, thank you. Thank you to my daughters, who celebrate with me when I finish the first draft all the way to when the first copy arrives in the mail, you are the best cheering squad a writer could hope for. To my mom for sharing your love of literature. To my dad, thank you for encouraging me to follow my passion. A big thanks to my brother for being my friend and for making me laugh like no one else.

I'm also indebted to many helpers for bringing this story to life. My friend Craig Isenberg, M.A., LMFT., has given me incredible insight into Cassidy's mind and motivations. Thank you for your time and for answering my endless questions. To Cathy Young for your kindness and support and for including me in the Wahine Kai surf club. Hopefully we'll actually surf waves together someday instead of just talk about it. Your friendship over the years means so much to me.

I'm also incredibly thankful for the support and expert skill of my editor, Jana Stojadinović, who has taught me so much, been my cheerleader, helped me brainstorm, and challenged me in all the very best ways. Thank you for giving this book your all.

Thank you to my readers and especially to my amazing ARC team! Stories are meant to be shared, and having your support means the world to me.

Finally, this story would never have happened had I not fallen in love with surfing. A big thank you goes out to our incredible oceans, beaches, and cultures around the world tied to the sport. Surfing is a constant reminder in patience, strength, and perseverance—a bit like writing. I'm forever grateful for the inspiration.

ABOUT THE AUTHOR

AMY WAESCHLE is the author of the #1 Amazon Bestselling suspense novel *Rescuing Reeve* and the Cassidy Kincaid Mysteries, the standalone novels *Feeding the Fire* and *Going Over the Falls*. She is a geologist by trade and a writer at heart. A challenging surf experience in Fiji inspired her first book, and she's been dreaming up stories ever since.

Amy likes to surf, run mountain trails, and spend time with her family. She loves to travel and has lived in Sicily, Sun Valley, the Alaskan bush, and in the back of her 1996 Isuzu Trooper. Currently, Amy and her husband live in Poulsbo, Washington with their two daughters. You can contact her at amywaeschle.com.

facebook.com/fictionbyamywaeschle

instagram.com/waeschleamy

pinterest.com/amywaeschle

Made in the USA
Monee, IL
09 January 2023

24869940R00125